EVER AFTER ALL

FIREWEED HARBOR SERIES

J.H. CROIX

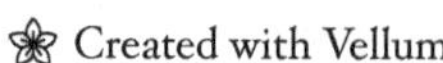 Created with Vellum

Chapter One

ROSIE

Las Vegas, Nevada

I stared at the ring on my finger. Oh. My. God.

Flashes of last night came back to me, partial scenes of intense moments.

Wyatt's starlight-blue eyes, dark as he held me. My hands gripping his shoulders. His weight over me, my name in a guttural cry. His name in my ragged voice, begging, pleading.

And why did I have a wedding ring on? I sifted through my memories. There was that pastor with the cowboy hat, a friendly guy. Me saying, "I do." Wyatt looking into my eyes, his expression serious, and repeating the words back to me.

I tried to focus on something else, anything else. The hot water rained down over me in this very nice shower. We're talking *nice*. Rainfall showerhead, jets on the walls, the works. I was grateful for the steaming hot water and the mist enveloping me. I needed to wash away my confusion.

I had a vague memory of Wyatt watching soap bubbles roll down over my skin and teasing me before tugging me out of the shower and back to the bed. Fuckity-fuck. I couldn't keep my brain on the right track.

I was panicking a little. Maybe not a little. It was full-blown panic here.

My body still felt sated with a few twinges here and there in very specific locations. I was sore in a way I hadn't been in a while. Actually, not since the last time I'd tumbled into bed with Wyatt Cannon. An unsettled sigh slipped through my lips.

Just when I was starting to accept my situation and try to formulate a plan, *any* plan, the bathroom door opened. *Fuck my life.*

Why didn't I lock the door?

Oh, probably because you freaked right the hell out when you woke up tangled up and naked with Wyatt.

The shower door opened, and he stepped in through the steam. Wyatt was a sight to behold. He had broad shoulders that tapered down to, well, muscled everything.

He turned to close the glass door behind him, giving me a nice view of his back. Sweet hell, the guy was in shape everywhere. When he turned back to face me and I saw a certain part of him lengthening, I felt the clench between my legs. I was already aroused because that was the kind of effect Wyatt had on me.

"Are you panicking yet?" he asked as he stepped under the water with me, his arms landing on the tile on either side of my shoulders. I looked up, thinking I needed to say something smart and quick to fake my way through this.

Instead, I answered honestly. "I'm panicking. Why

am I wearing a wedding band?" He stared at me through the blur of water falling around us. "Did we get married last night?"

Chapter Two

WYATT

One month later – Fireweed Harbor, Alaska

Did we get married last night? Rosie's question went round and round and round in my thoughts.

The answer, as it turns out, was yes.

We'd both had flights out of Vegas that morning. We hadn't had time to do anything other than rush to the airport. I supposed we could've canceled them, but we didn't.

We'd been back in Fireweed Harbor for a month and were busy pretending we weren't married. Rosie even pretended we hadn't even had that night together.

That whole "what happens in Vegas stays in Vegas" was trite for a reason. It's just I'd never expected to be living the fucking cliché.

I was on autopilot, turning into the parking lot behind Fireweed Industries headquarters. A moose was pawing the ground and snorting. I hit the brakes, bringing my truck to a jerking stop. I glanced in the direction of where she was to see a set of twin calves beside my older brother Blake's truck. Blake stood in his truck bed.

I chuckled to myself and slowly rolled past the mama moose. "Hop in!" I called as I rolled down the passenger side window, pulling close enough to prevent any moose from walking between the vehicles.

Blake caught my eyes. "Thanks!" A moment later, he climbed into the passenger seat. "I wasn't paying attention when I got out of my truck. Next thing I knew, mama moose was charging at me. Damn moose can cover some ground in no time!"

"Hazards of life in Alaska," I commented. "I'll park over there." I gestured to the parking area across from this one behind the brewery. We definitely needed to give this moose and her calves some time to get out of the parking lot. She pawed angrily at the ground as I continued rolling past her.

I slid my gaze to my brother. "Did you almost get trampled?"

"Closer call than I'd like. I was distracted when I got here and climbed out without checking. She was right there in the trees with her calves and charged at me. Thank fuck my reflexes are still good."

A moment later, I parked behind the brewery. Fireweed Industries was our family's corporation. Blake and I were the two family members who mostly worked in the old winery and brewery, the part of the business that started it all. Two generations ago, our grandmother had loved making batches of wine, beer, and mead. She started selling them at small fairs in Alaska and quickly realized she could make good money. She built the winery and brewery, opened a restaurant, and business boomed. It was at the time when oil and the money that followed it flowed in

Alaska. The family invested wisely in various holdings throughout the state—land, mining, oil rights, and so on.

The business leapfrogged into an international corporation with holdings all over the world. Distribution warehouses for wine, beer, and mead, as well as expansion from the oil and mining businesses. Our headquarters had been in Seattle for a while, but our oldest brother Rhys decided to move us back to where it all began. Being online made it much easier to do business from anywhere in the world. We had closed down our headquarters in Seattle and left a small satellite office there. We'd gradually filtered back to our hometown, the last of us being my twin brother, Griffin, and me. We'd been hotshot firefighters for the previous few years, and he still was. It started because we volunteered in high school at the local fire station and loved it. We'd wanted to spread our wings from our tiny town for a little while and sought the adventure of wildland firefighting.

Blake had finally persuaded me to return and take over the head brewing position because the prior one was moving to be closer to family. After we parked, Blake and I glanced over as we climbed out to see the moose and her calves had moved deeper into the cluster of alder trees by the parking area. The mama reached up to pull the branches down for her twin calves to eat.

"Maybe we should trim those alders," I commented as we walked across the parking lot into the back door.

Blake shrugged. "We could, but moose are all over town this time of year, no matter what."

"Why *are* there moose everywhere this time of year?" a voice asked.

Blake and I glanced up to see Fiona, his wife,

standing beside the small round table in the corner of the employee break room. A smile spread across Blake's face as he approached her. He ignored her question in favor of giving her a lingering kiss. He was seriously in love. He and Fiona met when she took the chef position at our restaurant. Years into marrying Fiona and the man was still ridiculously smitten.

I smiled between them. "Since your husband can't be bothered to answer your question, I will. Moose are around all the time, but we see them more now because their calves are young, and they're safer from the brown bears when they're closer to town."

Fiona's brows arched high as her eyes went wide. "Does that mean bears are going to come into town?"

Blake shook his head. "Not likely. They avoid people more. You're in more danger from a moose protecting her calves than a bear," he explained.

"Speaking of that, I just saved your husband's ass."

Fiona's wide eyes shifted to Blake. "What do you mean?"

Blake cast a sheepish smile. "I parked over there and wasn't looking when I got out. Didn't notice there was a mama and her twins right there."

Fiona sucked in a breath. "Blake!"

"I'm fine. See?" He gestured up and down his body. "I hopped in the back of my truck. I was perfectly safe."

"I love Alaska," she said. "But I prefer to see animals from a distance."

"There you are!" one of the line cooks said as he entered the break room.

He instantly distracted Fiona as he began explaining a problem with a delay in orders for the kitchen stock. She didn't even give Blake or me a backward glance as she hurried off.

"Let's get to work," I said.

He and I headed in opposite directions down the hallway as we walked out. The restaurant was toward the front of the building, with the brewery and distribution area at the back. We pushed through a set of double swinging doors, and the commotion of the kitchen carrying down the hallway was muted as the doors swung shut behind us.

"Speaking of supplies, am I keeping up on orders for you?" Blake asked.

"Absolutely. You make my job easy," I offered with a quick sideways glance.

It had been close to a year since I'd taken over as the head brewer. Blake managed the entire distribution operation for us. Technically, he was my boss. As our CEO, Rhys was also my boss. I was one of seven siblings. If you counted our eldest brother, we were eight, but he'd passed away when he was a senior in college. I was still in high school at the time. We'd later learned we had a half-brother born before our dad had even met our mom. Chase worked for us now too in one of our offices in Willow Brook, Alaska.

Like many families, we had a tangled history. Since we were a big family, there were more messy knots in that history. While we made most of our money from selling alcohol internationally, Jake drank himself to death in college. Alcohol poisoning was a nasty way to die. Blessedly, it didn't seem that any of the rest of us had an issue with alcohol. None of us drank much beyond the casual glass here and there.

We were stairsteps, with Jake first before he passed, then Rhys, Blake next, then a pair of twins—Adam, our CFO, and Kenan, who took care of whatever was needed at the corporation, as well as the brewery. The next set of twins was Griffin and me. He had moved back to Fireweed Harbor with me but was taking a position on the local hotshot firefighting crew. Last but definitely not least was our sister McKenna. She handled public relations for the corporation and everything that came along with it.

I enjoyed working with Blake. He was easygoing and hands-off as far as work went. Here at the brewery, we mostly stayed out of the fray of the rest of the corporation. I got to do what I loved, which was make beer, wine, and mead. We had our staples and best sellers, and Blake had given me free rein to do whatever else I wanted as far as new products, seasonal products, and so on.

"Hey, guys," Kenan said from behind us.

Glancing back, I grinned. "Hey, yourself. What's up?"

Kenan gestured to Blake, who had stopped in front of his office door. "Blake told me you might want to take a look at the extra bottling equipment we have. I'm headed out to the warehouse. Thought you might want to tag along?"

"Oh, that's right. He mentioned that." I glanced at my watch. "I have to do some training with a new guy we hired, but that's not for another two hours. Let's go take a look."

"Perfect," Kenan said. "Let's roll, then."

We waved goodbye to Blake, and a few minutes later, Kenan was driving through town. He was busy taking a call from Rhys about some construction issue in Willow Brook. We were revamping one of our mining facilities into a renewable energy facility there. I tuned out the one-sided conversation and soaked in the view as he drove.

Fireweed Harbor had the kind of beauty that imprinted on your soul. Towering, jagged mountain peaks, snow-covered even in the hottest months of the year, a glacier glittering nearby under the bright sun. The town was along the famed Inside Passage, one of Alaska's coastal jewels. The Inside Passage offered a travel route along a mostly protected waterway that snaked through the mountains and islands as it stretched through Canada to Alaska.

Thick rich, evergreen trees blanketed the lower slopes of the mountains. There were rocky stretches of coastline interspersed with gray sandy beaches with some of the best variety of colorful rocks you could find in the world. There was even the occasional lucky find of drops of lava that had rolled down the slopes of volcanoes and eventually made their way to the beach after freezing in the ocean waters.

Alaska formed the Northern part of what was known as the Ring of Fire, a tectonic belt of volcanoes in the Pacific Ocean that was comprised of almost two-thirds of the world's volcanoes. Those made for pretty views and the occasional lava rock on the beaches. Fireweed Harbor itself was a short distance away from Juneau and Skagway, situated, as the crow flew, a half hour away from Juneau.

As a plane flew, it was about a twenty-minute flight, give or take. No roads connected the towns in Southeast Alaska. The only way you could get here was by boat or plane. Cruise ships kept Fireweed Harbor busy during the cruise season. Like other towns in this area, we relied heavily on those tourist dollars and catered to them. Despite its sprawling geography, Alaska was a closely connected state for those who lived here year-round. Life here was on the edge of the wilderness, even in the larger cities.

In the southeastern part of the state, deer, moose, sea lions, seals, otters, massive brown bears, and more were all over the place. Outdoor activities were a staple of life all through the year. Our town was tucked into a little cove where the boat harbor was situated. The colorful and whimsical downtown area had bright signs, artsy shops, and excellent restaurants to meet the needs of the tourists and keep locals happy. Our family's corporation brought business and support into the town as well, donating to causes and creating jobs for the local community.

With the town tucked into the base of the mountains, it felt almost as if it were wrapped in an embrace. It was a special place to grow up, where it felt like the wild encircled you. Our population was small through winter and exploded with tourists in warmer months.

I'd left for college in Juneau with Griffin. After that, we'd trained to become hotshot firefighters in California before heading north to Fairbanks. Fairbanks was a solid daylong drive from Fireweed Harbor. I'd resisted moving home for years. But with more of the truth coming out about our family's tangled history, I'd finally decided to make the move.

I was jilted out of my reverie when Kenan slammed on his brakes. Looking ahead, I smiled at the black bear lumbering across the road with her two cubs behind her. We were on the outskirts of town now, near the warehouse where we stored supplies for the brewery, among other things.

"Seen many bears out at your house?" I asked after the bears disappeared into the trees.

"Just the other day, there was one in our backyard," he replied. "Speaking of houses, what's your plan?"

At the moment, Griffin and I were sharing one of our family's rentals. Griffin still wasn't sure he planned to stay long-term, while I was assessing options.

"I've been eyeing some land possibilities. I'll buy something already built too, if I find the right place."

Kenan turned off the main road onto a side road that led to the warehouse. We passed by another warehouse that belonged to the corporation. Among other things, property management and the like, we currently handle the contract for road maintenance in Fireweed Harbor. That warehouse had a garage for vehicle repairs for the multiple plows, trucks, and more. Beyond that was an empty field where some moose were feeding on some alder trees along the edges. A moment later, Kenan turned onto a gravel driveway.

"What are you looking for?" he asked.

"I want some privacy, but I don't really care all that much how far out of town it is. Peace and quiet aren't hard to find. Even in the rental, it's pretty quiet," I replied.

Kenan chuckled. "True."

A short while later, we were loading up equipment for the brewery. When we were done, Kenan closed the back of the truck and rested his hand on the tailgate. "I'm glad you're home. What took you so long?"

I held his gaze for a long beat, considering my words. But the illusion of perfection had been cracked wide open regarding our brother Jake. You'd think it would be easier to tell the truth about someone once they were dead, but my experience was the opposite. It was as if their death made it seem that it was not worth the trouble.

I took a quick breath. "Jake. He and I had it out right before he died. It just seemed easier to try not to crack the myth."

Kenan studied me for a few seconds. "Now that it's out for McKenna, do you feel like you don't have to stay quiet anymore?"

I cleared my throat before nodding. Jake had been a cruel bully to our sister. I'd called him out on it, and he died the next night. A part of me was still relieved he'd died, and I felt guilty and conflicted as hell over that. I'd never been able to see him the way our mother did.

"Do you want to talk about it?" Kenan prompted when I didn't reply.

I contemplated that before shaking my head. "Nah. I'm good."

I'd found my peace in making sure Jake understood he couldn't fucking hurt people I loved. I understood that he'd been traumatized, like all of us, by our grandfather. After our dad died, his parents had helped. Our grandmother was great. I still loved her even though I would never know just how many secrets she'd kept. But our grandfather had been verbally abusive to all of us and physically abusive mostly to Rhys and Jake. We would find out years after the fact that he'd also sexually abused Jake. All of that fed into Jake drinking himself to death.

I understood how trauma worked and how it could poison someone inside. Hurt people hurt people, so some people said. But that didn't really sit well for me. Lots of hurt people *didn't* hurt other people. Some of us learned what and who we didn't want to be from enduring pain meted out by others.

Jake had taken out most of his pain on McKenna. I'd called him out on it more than once. When I got big enough, I told him if he laid a fucking hand on her again, I'd make him pay. I'd never laid a hand on him. I just told him I would tell everyone the truth.

A piece of my heart ached for Jake because he'd carried the pain for all of us. That didn't make it okay that he took that pain and threw it like hot oil on others.

After a quiet moment, Kenan stepped to me and pulled me into a backslapping hug. "I'm just glad you're home. I'm here if you ever want or need to talk about anything."

"I know it."

My chest loosened a little, knowing I wasn't hiding anymore.

Chapter Three

ROSIE

"Which room?" I asked.

"Exam room two," Harry, one of the nurses on duty, replied as he hurried past me.

The emergency room department at Fireweed Harbor's small hospital was busy in the summer. During the quieter months of the year, we could count on some slow nights with bursts of excitement. Come summer, when the town's population quadrupled, the pace was relentless. With fishing hooks flying through the air and accidental wildlife encounters, not only were we busy but every day was also interesting. I never wondered when my shift would end because I didn't have time to look at the clock.

As the supervisory nurse on duty, I was technically in charge, but we all knew what the hell we were doing here. When it was busy, it was like watching an engine at work with one lever pulling the next. In this case, I was the lever available for the newest emergency. I had just finished helping stabilize a grandfather, who was still shocked he'd had a minor heart attack. He insisted he did everything perfectly as far as diet and exercise. Meanwhile, his wife, who clearly loved him, had explained to me that his idea of taking good care of himself was more aspirational than actual.

I almost ran past the exam room, catching myself at the last minute before knocking lightly on the door. "Come in!" the medical assistant called out.

When I walked in, I glanced over to see Wyatt. *My husband.* I reflexively fingered the ring on a necklace under my scrubs. I couldn't bring myself to wear it on my hand, but for some inexplicable reason, I couldn't *not* wear it. I still couldn't figure out why I hadn't filed for divorce.

Wyatt's blue eyes met mine as he gave me a sheepish smile. He sat before me with a big fish hook sticking out of his shoulder.

"Is that a halibut hook?" I asked.

I glanced over at the medical assistant who was biting his lip and trying really hard not to laugh. Meanwhile, Wyatt let out a resigned sigh. "Go ahead and laugh. I won't take offense."

The med assistant Danny finally let loose a chuckle, his eyes twinkling as he met my gaze. "It *is* a halibut hook. Wyatt tells me he's a fishing expert and isn't sure how this happened."

I had to bite the insides of my cheeks to keep from laughing myself. When I looked back at Wyatt, he shrugged. He circled his hand in the air. "Just laugh. You know you want to. Better get it out so you don't have to hold it in the whole time."

I finally laughed as I approached him. "I'm sure you've already told Danny, and I can read the notes, but how about you let me know what happened? I'm dying to hear."

When I stopped maybe a foot away where he sat on the exam table, it felt like the equivalent of walking into a force field. It locked around us, a vibrating force so powerful I could feel it in my bones. I ignored the way my pulse galloped along like a happy pony let out to pasture.

"I was fishing, and... just poor focus on my part. Blake and I are teaching Lia how to catch halibut, and I should've been paying better attention."

Lia was Wyatt's niece and newer to Alaska. She and her mother had only moved here a few years prior. I bit the insides of my cheeks again as I nodded, keeping my gaze solemn.

"Can I take a look?" I asked.

"That's exactly what he told me," Danny chimed in as he stood from the small wheeled desk where the computer monitor was mounted with an adjustable keyboard. "I have all his stats in there. Blood pressure is normal, nothing out of the ordinary. It looks like he'll need a few stitches. Do you want me to stay?" He glanced toward Wyatt for this.

"Are you asking because you're worried that I don't feel safe with Rosie?" Wyatt looked genuinely befuddled.

"Technically, yes," Danny replied.

Wyatt rolled his eyes. "Safe and sound. Trust her completely."

"If you need anything, just page me," Danny added before he left.

A moment later, it was just Wyatt and me in this small exam room. This was actually the first time we'd been together alone since that fated morning. I'd woken up married with my body sore from head to toe in all kinds of delicious ways.

He waggled his brows when I met his gaze again. I cleared my throat and forced myself to focus.

"So, uh, you got a fish hook in your shoulder, and

—" I gestured to the side of his head where a piece of gauze was in place.

Wyatt winced. "I bonked my head on the corner of the boat windshield. It's nothing, but it hurt like hell at the time."

"I bet." As I studied him, I could see he was trying to keep his pain at bay. A light sheen of sweat coated his forehead, and his skin was pale under the bright glare of the overhead lights. "Are you okay?" I asked gently.

He cleared his throat and nodded. "I'd just like to get the hook out of my shoulder and get stitched up. Will you be doing that?" He looked a little worried, and my heart felt pinched.

My usual calm, dispassionate approach was feeling wobbly. It wasn't that I didn't care about my patients, but we had to keep our emotions at a distance in this work. Otherwise, we'd be sobbing some nights, and that wouldn't usually help patients stay calm. In this case, Wyatt would be fine. He *was* fine. But no matter what I tried to tell myself, I cared about him. An awful lot.

I took a slow breath and turned away. "Let me see..." I spun the computer monitor in my direction, quickly scanning his info. "It says here you rated your pain at a four?"

When I arched a brow in question, he shrugged, clearly not thinking about the hook buried in one of his shoulders. He immediately winced, his breath hissing in through his teeth. "Well, now it's maybe a seven."

"Can I persuade you to take something for your pain? It says in there that you said ibuprofen would do the trick."

"It will," he said firmly. "I'm scared of those pain meds. They ruin lives."

"It's a reasonable fear, but they are warranted in this situation. Taking a single dose is safe. You have a giant hook in your shoulder, Wyatt," I pointed out.

He rolled his eyes again and heaved a sigh. "Just tell me how to get out of here as quickly as possible."

"I will do my absolute best to make that happen," I replied, feeling my heart soften as I studied him. This strong, tough man, a hotshot firefighter wrapped in a muscled body that I knew intimately, seemed vulnerable. The hospital wasn't fun for anyone. In a case like this, it was incredibly frustrating. When things were dicey, people tended to have a little more patience. Wyatt would be fine, but he definitely needed stitches. Entering the hospital was like hopping on a conveyor belt. It was a one-way journey, and you had to stay on it until you made it all the way through to the other side.

I tipped my head to the side. "You're going to be fine. We'll get that hook out, the doctor will come and stitch you up, and you'll be off. We'll send you home with some antibiotics to prevent infection."

"Can't you do all of this?" he asked, startling me as I moved to turn away and felt his hand curl around my wrist. His touch was like a flame encircling my wrist.

"There's a lot I can do, but the doctor has to handle the stitches. Plus..." Pausing, I cleared my throat. "We have a personal relationship. I probably shouldn't be the one handling this."

Wyatt was quiet as he stared at me. "This is Fireweed Harbor. You have a personal relationship with half the damn town."

I pressed my lips together. "I know. This isn't that

big of a deal. But the doctor's the one who needs to stitch you up, not me."

I moved to go again, and Wyatt tightened his grip on my wrist. His touch was so light that the shift was incremental. "What is it?" I asked.

"I think you know," he pointed out.

"I know?" Heat flashed into my cheeks.

"How long do you plan to ignore me?"

"I'm not ignoring you, Wyatt," I ground out. "We just have to figure out this whole divorce thing."

"Why?" he pressed.

"Wyatt!" I was exasperated.

"Tell me you've had it as good with anyone else," he said flatly.

My pulse hummed along at a breakneck pace, and I tried to take a steadying breath, but I could barely get any air into my lungs. I wanted to lie—I really, *really* did—but found that I couldn't.

"Let's see how it goes," he said.

"See how what goes?"

"Us," he said, his voice clear and decisive.

While I was shying away from the situation, Wyatt was running at it, full bore.

It felt like my heart might fly straight out of my chest. I took a shaky breath. "See how it goes?"

It might have seemed like I was hedging, avoiding, and playing dumb, but I actually wasn't. I didn't even know what to think. See how *what* went? Our absolutely impulsive marriage? Our insanely hot night?

I was embarrassed that I couldn't remember getting married, except for a few vague details. Yet, while maybe not completely clear, my memory of our night together was vivid and visceral. I could feel it in my body, remember his dark eyes, the feel of his weight over me, the feel of him filling me and bringing me to climax after climax.

As I held his gaze, I realized he was serious.

I had avoided admitting my feelings to myself for years. That night in Vegas wasn't our first rodeo. We had a fling one week before I started nursing school. That week had been impossible to forget.

Dating was like picking my way through a wasteland of assholes. It seemed like every guy just wanted benefits. They didn't even want to be friends. Even that was too much to ask.

That week with Wyatt had sent my expectations skyrocketing up and over into the stratosphere. Every attempt with any guy since had been a huge disappointment. I felt like I was broken. I would sigh and go home and wonder what the hell I was doing. Conveniently, my job was an easy distraction, and I was always busy. I could sign up for extra shifts whenever I wanted. I could tell myself I was too busy for a relationship.

Ever since the pandemic, health care had been caught in a brutal cycle of staff leaving. It had started before that with the misery of insurance companies denying much-needed health care left and right. Since the pandemic, the pace of staff leaving had picked up. Despite all that, I still loved my job.

I kept busy working and could forget about wishing I could find a relationship. I didn't like to think much about why I had my own reasons for struggling to connect emotionally with someone.

"Rosie," Wyatt prompted. His voice was soft and gruff, and my heart thumped unsteadily.

I had tried to tell myself it was nothing more than a fluke of wild chemistry with him. Since he'd lived away from Fireweed Harbor for years, I didn't have to face him often, but now that he'd moved back, I kept bumping into him. Not only was our hometown small but our social circles were pretty much the same. My friends were married to his brothers. McKenna, his only sister, was one of my closest friends.

It felt like every time I turned around, Wyatt was there. Then Vegas happened. I felt the warmth of that cheap wedding band against my breastbone, where it rested behind my scrubs. I didn't even know why I was wearing it.

"What?" I pressed.

"It's not like Vegas was our first round," he pointed out.

He reached for my hand, and I didn't resist. His touch was warm, and his thumb brushed along the outer edge of my palm as he studied me. I felt exposed with his attention so focused on me.

"I think it's worth seeing how it goes. If things work out, well, we don't have to plan a wedding." The way his lips curled up at one corner sent heat in a swirl through me and tingles radiating outward.

My belly felt ticklish, and I felt knocked off balance inside.

When I didn't reply, he added, "We can get divorced if you insist."

I swallowed. I didn't understand why I hadn't pushed this divorce thing sooner. Instead, I was trying to pretend Wyatt didn't exist, trying to pretend we hadn't had the hottest nights *ever* together.

"So what do we do?" I was a little shocked that I asked that. His eyes widened slightly. "I'm not ready to tell people what happened," I added quickly.

"What are we keeping secret?" he pressed.

"Our marriage." I was flustered. With heat pooling

in my belly and my skin prickling all over, the feel of the flush on my cheeks only added to my state.

He lifted his other hand, his fingers lightly pressing over the ring hiding behind my scrubs. "Why are you wearing this?"

I tried to take a deep breath, but all I got was a tiny sip of air. "I don't know." I hated how Wyatt tended to draw honesty out of me. Desperate for distraction, I pointed out, "You know, you have a fish hook in your shoulder, and we really need to take care of that."

He didn't look away as he nodded slowly. His hand dropped away from my chest. He reached under his shirt to pull out his wedding band on a silver chain. I licked my lips before whispering, "Oh."

He tucked it back under his shirt before pulling me a little closer. With him seated on the exam table, his eyes were a little higher than mine. He palmed my cheek. Before I could think, I felt the shock of his lips on mine. His kiss started slow and lingering. His tongue glided across the seam of my lips as they opened to him, and I let out a needy sigh. I was desperate for him. I took a step closer, my hand pressing on his chest as our tongues tangled.

We broke apart, and I could barely breathe as I stared at him.

"Think about it," he said, his dark gaze boring into mine.

Chapter Four

WYATT

"You're good to go," the doctor said.

I glanced over at the doctor. I was a little out of it. They'd given me a sedative to help me relax while she stitched me up. She was very polite and as matter-of-fact as one could get. Although she looked barely out of med school, I appreciated her calm, practical bedside manner.

"How's your pain?" she asked.

"Well, I can't feel a thing because you put that numbing spray on it," I pointed out.

She smiled a little. She hadn't even blinked at the fish hook in my shoulder and had shared that when she was younger and out fishing at her family's fishing camp, she had once gotten a hook deep in her forearm and showed me the scar.

"I promise your scar won't be as obvious," she'd offered wryly.

Even though I'd been woozy, we'd spent most of the time chatting about our favorite fishing areas while she stitched me up. Like me, she had grown up in Alaska. While I had grown up here in Fireweed

Harbor, she had grown up on the outskirts of Juneau. As a member of the Tlingit tribe, she had spent much of her childhood fishing in tribal areas. She had shared that she was thrilled to get a job at the hospital in Fireweed Harbor, where her grandparents were originally from.

"The numbing spray will wear off, probably in an hour or so. I'm sending you home with a prescription for some pain medication. You're going to need it. Trust me, that hook was deep in your shoulder. You can expect some soreness for a week or so."

"I don't want to take pain medication. I hate that shit. It makes me feel fuzzy, and I already feel fuzzy," I pointed out.

She nodded. "Understood, but I recommend taking some to help with the pain. Honestly, just a day or two should be good enough." Her eyes bounced to the clock on the wall. "I have to move along, but a nurse will come in to clear you for discharge."

"Will it be Rosie?" My question slipped out.

The doctor eyed me for a beat before she replied, "Probably not. She's dealing with another emergency." Clearly, my poker face wasn't at its best. Her eyes twinkled. "It's obvious you like Rosie."

Like didn't even come close to capturing how I felt about Rosie.

"Rosie is awesome. I've known her forever."

The doctor's pager beeped. "I really do have to go. Watch out for infection. You have a prescription for antibiotics and pain meds. Between the two, the antibiotics are probably more important. We did our best to flush the wound, but fish hooks can have nasty stuff on them."

I blamed what I said next on the sedatives that

hadn't completely worn off. "Okay. I love Rosie. We're married. She doesn't want anybody to know."

The doctor gave me a puzzled look and nodded along. "You take care and don't leave until you're cleared for discharge."

A few minutes later, another nurse was in the room. She reviewed my discharge instructions and informed me I couldn't drive myself home.

"Why not?" I demanded.

"Is there anyone you can call for a ride?" she asked, not even deigning to answer my ridiculous question.

"Rosie. She's here. When does she get off?"

I wasn't clear on the details, but a short while later, Rosie walked me out of the hospital. "Why did you tell the doctor we were married?" she asked as she guided me out into the parking lot.

"Because we are!"

"Oh my God," she muttered.

I was pretty sure Rosie wanted to be pissed off at me. But once she got me situated in the passenger seat of her car and reached around me to buckle my seat belt, she met my gaze and shook her head slowly with a bemused smile. "You are loopy."

The drive from the hospital to the small house I was sharing with my twin brother was short. I reached over the console to try to hold her hand, but my aim fell short as she turned off the car. "Think about it," I repeated.

Rosie looked over at me. "You're out of it, Wyatt. I'm going to walk you inside. If you tell Griffin we're married, I'll tell him that you're crazy, just like I told the doctor."

A few minutes later, she escorted me into the house. My brother stood at the kitchen counter. "Where the hell have you been?" he asked.

"I got a fish hook in my shoulder. Didn't Blake call you?"

Griffin looked from Rosie to me as she guided me over to the couch. "He's still a little out of it from the sedative they gave him," she explained when I plunked down on the couch. "The effects should wear off soon."

Griffin nodded as he approached us. "Blake texted, but I don't think I got all the details. He mentioned a fish hook, but I didn't think it was a big deal."

"I drove myself to the hospital." I patted my newly stitched-up shoulder before wincing. "Ouch!"

Rosie rolled her eyes before she fished two prescription bottles out of her purse. "Where did those come from?" I asked.

"Hospital." Griffin stopped beside the couch, and she handed them to him. "His pain meds and his antibiotics," she explained. "If anything comes up, call me or the hospital. He has a follow-up appointment to get his stitches removed in ten days."

Moments later, Rosie was gone, and Griffin was looking down at me.

"How's your wife?" he asked with a grin as soon as the door closed behind her.

I smiled up at him. "I love her."

My thoughts were sluggish but painfully honest.

Griffin sat down across from me in the chair, his gaze bemused. "I know you do, but I don't think Rosie knows that. What are you going to do about it?"

Chapter Five

ROSIE

"Dammit," I muttered.

I lowered my hand, setting my eyeliner on the counter in my bathroom. I lifted a piece of tissue and slid it carefully under my eye, where I'd just smeared it at the wrong angle.

At least for this task, my shaky nerves didn't matter. I took an unsteady breath. I knew what was wrong. My nerves had been shot to pieces ever since that night in Vegas. Ever since I'd woken up with a wedding band on. Ignoring Wyatt didn't seem to be helping matters. The only time I could focus was when I was at work, blessedly busy dealing with one emergency after another.

Two weeks had passed since Wyatt kissed me at the hospital. I had very purposely made sure I rearranged my schedule so I wasn't on duty the day he'd been scheduled to get his stitches removed. I didn't want him to know that ever since he'd put his suggestion in the air between us, I could hardly stop thinking about it. My feelings were a jumbled mess. He wanted me to give us a chance? What the hell?

When I had my little fling with Wyatt, life had been much simpler. I'd been fresh out of college and about to start my nursing program. I'd felt ready to face the world. The week with him had been beyond amazing, but it felt like a space out of time. He'd left to fight fires in the wilderness, and I'd started nursing school. I'd hardly seen him for years.

Nobody had measured up to him, at least not when it came to the sexy times. I didn't like to let myself think about the emotions. Every time I did, I mentally shied away. Maybe I'd fantasized about all kinds of things with him, but a little perspective went a long way. For the past few years, I didn't have much time to think about emotions. In some ways, I'd been relieved that none of my dating options had worked out.

I was busy taking care of my father and up to my eyeballs in stress. My friends knew a little bit about my stress, but I didn't want to complain. It felt like everything had snowballed so fast I could hardly keep track. My mom had died when I was a little girl, and my dad had stepped up to the plate in a big way. He'd worked his ass off to scramble things together. I'd been the older sister to my little brother and helped as much as I could at home even though my dad never asked me to help.

Now, my dad, who had seemed indestructible to me all of my life, was slipping. His memory seemed to skip like an old record on occasion. He lost track of details sometimes and had developed issues with his balance after an ear infection that he ignored for too long. My little brother, by eight years, had just dropped out of college and returned home to Fireweed Harbor. Between trying to take care of him and constantly worrying about my dad, I felt completely overwhelmed all the time.

I heard the sound of a door opening and closing and hurried out of the bathroom. I could get through the day without eyeliner. I lived in a small house on my father's property and came over often in the morning to check on him. I'd forgotten to put on eyeliner at home so had pulled it out of my purse here to take care of.

Rushing down the hall, I found my dad in the kitchen, staring at the coffee maker.

"Good morning, Dad," I said, my voice chipper.

He glanced over his shoulder, a smile spreading across his face. "Hey, Rosie girl."

My brother, Brent, walked in, running a hand through his messy hair.

My dad turned, stumbling on his feet a little bit. "Well, look who made it home last night." My dad's voice was good natured. At twenty-two, my brother liked to be out and about at night.

I knew my brother was struggling with something he wasn't telling me, but all I could do was wait. After he dropped out of college last year, he'd done some commercial fishing, which wasn't easy. The schedule was all over the place, with stretches of no work interspersed with grueling work. Between that, he was bouncing around doing odd jobs. He resisted working for my dad at his hardware store even though it would really help my dad.

"What's up with the coffee?" my brother asked, gesturing to the empty coffee pot.

"I think it died," my dad said.

"Seriously?" My brother crossed over and tapped it lightly with his hand. He did all the things, unplugging it, and then plugging it back in. After a few tries to get it to turn on, he glanced back at my dad. "It died."

My dad chuckled. "That's what I thought. Should we go get coffee in town together?"

"I'll take you to town, Dad," I said, just as my brother replied, "I actually have to get into work. Kenan Cannon told me to be there today at eight sharp. I'll see you guys around."

Without another word, my brother was gone. I didn't miss the detail that his eyes dodged mine. Aside from the usual life of a twenty-two-year-old—working, hanging out with his friends, and being out later than I preferred—something was going on. But I had enough to worry about. I couldn't fix it until I knew what it was, so the worry and anxiety just churned along inside.

Ever since my dad came home with my little baby brother after I said goodbye to my mom at the hospital, I'd lived with anxiety. I swallowed through the tightness in my chest and throat and went out to start my car. During the years after my mom had died, my dad had made some strategic decisions, including building the small rental house on his property where I lived. He stayed in the main house, where my brother recently moved in with him. Sometimes I felt like they were constantly rubbing each other the wrong way, creating static electricity in the air between them. Blessedly, my dad was less worried than I was about my brother.

A short drive later, my father held the door for me at Spill the Beans Café. This coffee shop was the town's nerve center. Beyond the best coffee to be found, delicious baked goods, sandwiches, and more, the two owners, Hazel and Phyllis, were longtime best friends. They knew everything about any gossip in town. I didn't remember a time when the café wasn't here. It had opened sometime during my childhood.

During the cold winter days and long nights, the sign, soft pink with coffee beans spilled underneath, was a beacon for local residents.

As soon as we stepped inside and the door swung shut behind us with a cheery little chime announcing our arrival, my dad smiled. "They made the dark chocolate and almond croissants."

"You sure about that?" I teased.

"I can smell them, and I'm getting one. What about you?"

We walked together to get in the back of the line. "I'm in the mood for something more savory," I replied.

My father didn't even hear my answer as he was already chatting with Derek, Jack Hamilton's brother. If Jack was here, that likely meant McKenna was. A quick glance around and I found McKenna with Tessa and Quinn, some of my closest friends. I waved over at them.

When we got to the counter, my father spoke again, "I'll cover your coffee. I'm sitting with Derek, though. He's taking me home."

I smiled at Derek. "You sure about that?"

Derek's eyes twinkled with his smile. "Sure thing. Your dad and I have bonded. Although he doesn't have cancer, he goes to the same clinic as me for his rehab. We hang out in the waiting room together."

"So I've heard. I'm glad you two can keep each other company." I nudged my dad lightly with my shoulder. Just as I contemplated whether to ask Derek about how his cancer treatment was going, my dad offered, "He's kicking cancer's ass."

"Good to hear," I replied.

Derek waggled his brows. "I've even gained some weight. Ten whole pounds."

Considering that Derek was painfully thin, that was good news. We ordered, and my dad gestured toward my friends as he walked to a table with Derek. I crossed the café, stopping beside the table where my friends were seated. "Mind if I sit with you all?"

"As if you need to ask," McKenna said as she smiled up at me. "Quinn already stole you a chair from another table."

I slipped into the chair Quinn patted, dropping my purse on the ground and hanging my jacket over the back. Once I was seated, I took a swallow of coffee. "So how are we this morning?" I asked the table at large.

"You have to see this." McKenna pulled her phone up, tapping on her screen, and showing me a picture of her cat, Snowy. In the photo, Jack had Snowy tucked into his jacket. "He walks around the house with her like that. It's ridiculous."

"It's adorable," I replied. "So how is married life?"

McKenna let out a contented sigh. "It's really great."

"Marriage turns out to be pretty sweet," Tessa chimed in.

Quinn laughed as she glanced around the table. "And you two were so opposed to marriage once upon a time."

All eyes turned to me. "What?" I took a quick bite of my spinach-and-feta-stuffed pastry. Chewing was an excellent reason not to talk.

Of course, the bite I took was too big, and I almost choked, resulting in Quinn patting me between the shoulder blades. "Are you okay?" she asked.

After I managed to swallow and clear my throat, I nodded. "I'm fine."

I was relieved when Hazel stopped by our table to check on us. "How are we doing, girls?"

She had a small tray in one hand and began picking up a few empty plates at the table.

"Are we really girls?" I teased as I smiled up at Hazel.

"To me, you are. I am..." She paused briefly before adding, "Over seventy. Once you clear fifty, every female under forty is a girl."

Tessa's eyes twinkled. "How do you figure that, though?"

"Well, I'm old enough to be your mother, so I can say that," Hazel replied archly.

Just then, the door to the café opened, and Wyatt and Griffin walked in together. Hazel glanced over. I was relieved nobody happened to be looking at me when Wyatt's gaze arced around the café before landing on me. It felt like a camera wobbling and coming into focus before locking into place. Electricity jolted through me in a fiery-hot sizzle.

Hazel smiled and waved with one hand before looking back at us. "Those two. Last Cannon men standing. And they're firefighters." She waggled her brows. "We should start a betting pool."

"On what?" I couldn't help but ask.

"Who's going to be the last one to fall in love? Because it's got to be somebody," Hazel explained.

"Well, they're twins," Tessa pointed out. "Maybe it'll happen at the same time."

Hazel shrugged just before her sharp, perceptive gaze landed on me. I knew instantly she was aware of something. Heat rolled in a slow wave through me. I took another bite of my pastry, which was a delicious distraction.

Hazel moved along and returned to the counter

when another rush of customers came in. I silently crossed my fingers and toes, hoping Wyatt didn't come over to our table.

But he did because, of course. His sister was with me, along with two sisters-in-law. There was no reason for him not to say hello, especially since Griffin was with him. When they finally made their way to our table, I almost choked on my food again, but I managed to finesse my way through it this time. Of course then, I had to go and ask the stupidest question. "How's your shoulder?"

"What happened to your shoulder?" Tessa immediately asked.

"Got a fish hook in it. It was kind of deep." Wyatt's gaze met mine, and my skin prickled with awareness.

"How do you know about that?" Quinn asked.

I took a gulp of coffee. "Because I was at the hospital when he came in." I hoped my tone sounded casual. "How is it anyway?"

"I got my stitches out last week. Just a little bit of soreness left," Wyatt explained.

"He told me I can't punch him in the shoulder yet, though," Griffin teased.

"Well, I would hope not," McKenna said.

I took another swallow of coffee and the last bite of my croissant. Kenan came into the café, of course, because the Cannon family was freaking huge. There were seven of them. He didn't even go to the counter first. He came straight to our table to give Quinn a lingering kiss. He was so whipped. They'd been together over two years now, and the guy still practically drooled over her.

The conversation carried on around me, and I

focused on my coffee and picking at the crumbs on my plate.

"Rosie," someone said.

I glanced up to see Kenan looking at me. "Yes?"

"I was just saying your brother's doing great with us," Kenan replied.

"Good to hear."

"I was telling him he might want to look into hotshot training since he likes working outside," Kenan added.

Griffin chimed in, "I'll give him a call. They have a new round of training coming up in a few months."

"Do they do training here?" I asked curiously.

Wyatt and Griffin nodded in unison. Griffin was still a hotshot firefighter, but Wyatt had recently transitioned away from that to take the head brewer position at Fireweed Winery for their family.

"Well, that would be great. He's bounced around between jobs," I said.

"Most people bounce around between jobs when they're his age," Griffin replied. "I'll get his number from Kenan and give him a call."

While I would worry about my brother doing a high-risk job like hotshot firefighting, it would be a relief for him to have a job that maybe he liked. My worry about my little brother was a constant simmer in my thoughts. It always had been. A little while later, I left because I needed to get to work myself. I said my goodbyes and slipped away, relieved Wyatt was occupied in conversation with my dad, Derek, Kenan, and Griffin. They'd started discussing something to do with hunting.

I was checking my phone messages before I drove away when there was a tap on my window. I glanced up to see Wyatt waiting on the other side. His breath frosted the air, and his blue eyes were bright. I was instantly hot all over. Because that was what seemed to happen whenever I looked at Wyatt.

I tapped the button to roll down my window. It would've been rude not to do that, but I also couldn't help myself.

"Hi," I said after clearing my throat.

"Hey. I was wondering if you thought about what I asked you?"

Chapter Six

WYATT

Rosie blinked at me. Her cheeks were flushed a pretty shade of pink, and I wanted to lean through the window and kiss her. I knew that wouldn't fly, so I simply waited.

"I have," she finally said, which surprised me. I had expected her to dodge. "I don't know how to do this. I'm staying in the extra house on my dad's property because he needs a little help right now, so—"

I paused, considering our options. "Locals' night is tomorrow at the winery. Find me there. We'll figure it out."

She held my gaze for another long beat before nodding. "Okay."

I walked away, with energy and anticipation humming through my body.

———

Griffin threw a quick smile my way. "So what exactly are you planning to do about Rosie?"

Even though Griffin knew we had married in a

drunken haze in Vegas, even though he knew I kind of had a thing for her and had for years, even though he knew I was in love with her—because, apparently, I'd fessed up to that when I'd been all doped up from anesthesia after the stitches—he knew I had no clue about what to do.

"You have no idea." He was teasing, but his gaze sobered after a moment.

"I definitely don't," I said flatly.

I let out a sigh as I turned and finished adjusting one of the valves on a tank in the brewing area. When I straightened, I glanced around the room. I had resisted coming home. Not because I didn't love Fire-weed Harbor. I did. And I loved my family. But we'd been through some shit together growing up. The collective worship of our oldest brother Jake, who had died over a decade ago, had grated on me. It wasn't even a conscious choice, more that life had naturally drawn me away and offered a convenient excuse.

I was of the mind that when you came from a really small town like this, going away for a little while sometimes made the most sense. Sometimes you needed to understand what you were missing.

When the opportunity had come up to take over the brewing management, something I enjoyed, I was glad to come back. I couldn't have planned the timing, but finally, most of the truth had come out about our brother.

The brewing room here felt like mine. It was a place where I could lose myself in tinkering. I turned and took a few steps, resting my hips against the table and curling my hands on the edge.

"Well, you've already made the commitment," he pointed out. "Now you just have to convince Rosie it's worth keeping."

"I know. What's the plan for when you'll start with the crew here?" I didn't want to keep dwelling on Rosie.

Griffin was taking a position on a hotshot expansion crew based out of here. "Jack is keeping me up to speed, and it looks like I'll be able to get started in the next few months. It's not sure that the crew will stay based in Fireweed Harbor, though. Jack plans to switch to the local crew if the state moves it to Willow Brook."

"Well, if you end up in Willow Brook, you'll be near Archer and Chase." I was referring to our cousin and half-brother who lived in that small Alaskan town. "You know Kenan's going to lean on you heavy to work for us," I added.

Griffin's lips quirked at the corners. "I know. I'll make that call when I'm ready."

Just then, as if on cue, Kenan came striding through the doorway. "Hey, guys."

"Hey, hey," I replied, just as Griffin asked, "What's up?"

"You guys have a few minutes? I could use some help unloading a few things that came in for the restaurant."

I pushed away from the table just as Griffin began walking toward Kenan. "At your service," he replied.

We walked with Kenan down the hallway. "What do you have for the restaurant?" I asked as we turned into the employee break room.

"Fiona is making some improvements in the kitchen. We've got a crew coming over to install some things today, so we shut down for the morning," he explained.

"We need to hustle then," I replied.

Moments later, we were hefting the new kitchen

equipment from where it had been deposited just outside the building on a pallet. A crew was moving swiftly to get things installed.

"Is there a reason you chose to do this on a Wednesday?" I teased lightly.

Kenan shook his head. "No, other than it's when it got delivered, and we didn't want to leave it outside. The guys assured me they would have it installed and ready to roll in time for a late opening for lunch. Fiona has everything prepped for locals' night already."

Blake happened to come walking into the kitchen and caught the tail end of our conversation. "Because she always does," he offered.

Kenan grinned over at him. "She always does."

Just then, our sister McKenna walked into the kitchen from the back hallway. "Oh!" she exclaimed. "That is a shiny stove."

I chuckled as I straightened from setting it down. Kenan and I carefully adjusted it. "Who moved everything last night to make room in here?" I asked.

"We paid the crew to stay late. They wanted to. They're all motivated because they want this new stuff," he explained.

Within about a half hour, we had carried in two new grills for the line cooks and the new oven for Fiona's baked goods. Everybody pitched in and helped. Fiona and David arrived in the midst of it. David was our longtime chef and had handed over chef duties to Fiona about two years ago to focus solely on the administrative part of managing the restaurant. He was extra busy these days as we were opening up a brewery and winery in the Willow Brook area where our half-brother and cousin lived.

We collectively high-fived when it was finished. McKenna rested her hands on her hips as she smiled at me, literally beaming. "I am *so* glad you and Griffin are back home."

"Yeah?" I teased with a grin.

"You know it!" she said before throwing her arms around me in an impulsive hug.

Blake pulled me into a backslapping hug for good measure. When I stepped back and glanced around at my siblings, I couldn't help the smile that formed. It felt good to be here.

All of us had been scattered for a period of years, including college, life, and so on. Once Rhys made the call to relocate the corporate headquarters back here, most of us gradually returned, except for me and Griffin. I had been thinking of coming back. After McKenna had opened up about what had happened with Jake, it felt like I didn't have to keep that secret for her anymore.

I still experienced twinges of guilt, but maybe I could find a way to banish those.

"You'll be at locals' night tonight, right?" Blake prompted as we began to filter out of the room.

"Of course. Isn't it required?" I teased.

Kenan chuckled at my side as we walked down the hallway toward the break room. "It's a soft requirement, but it's worth it."

"No argument from me. Good food, good drinks, and plenty of friends and family."

"And you can catch up on the local gossip," David added as he followed us into the break room.

"I don't care about the gossip," I said.

"You *are* the gossip," Blake announced.

"Me?"

"You and Griffin. You're new to town," he replied.

"Uh, we grew up here," I pointed out.

David waggled his brows. "That's not the point. You recently moved back, and you're both single."

Griffin happened to walk in from the back door just as David replied. He caught my eyes but didn't say a word.

I rolled my eyes. "I'm not looking."

I was very much *not* single. But aside from me and Rosie, only the doctor I'd confessed to in my loopy state when I got stitches and Griffin knew. If Rosie found out he knew, she'd be beyond furious.

Locals' night at Fireweed Winery was packed that evening. The restaurant held these weekly throughout the year to cater to the locals with special prices on food and free samples of beer, wine, and mead. During the summer months, it was even busier because we didn't bother to distinguish between tourists and locals. Anyone who showed up got at least one free drink.

I weaved through the crowded area near the bar, glancing around until I spied Rhys standing with his wife, Haven. Our mother, Kenan and Quinn, Blake and Fiona, and Adam and Tessa were all there. As usual, the family was out in force.

I slipped in beside my mother, leaning down to give her a quick kiss on the cheek. "Hey, Mom."

She beamed up at me, slipped her hand through my elbow, and squeezed. "I'm so glad you're here."

"Mom, just to point out, I've been here for almost a year now."

"I know, but I had to wait extra long for you and

Griffin to finally move back to town. I'm relieved you're not going out and fighting fires anymore. Now we just have to convince your twin to stop doing that."

"He will when he's ready," I said lightly.

Someone said something to my mother, and she released my elbow, immediately drawn into a conversation with Fiona and Quinn about the kitchen renovation at the restaurant.

Rhys caught my eyes, lifting his chin in acknowledgment. "How's it going over at the brewery?"

"I love it," I replied honestly.

"Good to hear." Rhys had his arm looped around Haven's waist. He'd been the first of us to settle down. They already had a toddler-aged son as well. As far as I could tell, Rhys was still deep in the honeymoon phase of being in love with Haven.

She smiled at me after she took a swallow of her mead. She held up the bottle and wiggled it in her hand. "I love this new flavor."

"It's a blueberry-blackberry combo. I ran it as a special to see how it sells."

"I think you should make it a permanent product," Haven said.

McKenna appeared at her side, immediately joining in. "That's what I said! I love it."

Blake chimed in, "It's selling really well. We usually make more money if we offer them on a limited basis."

Haven sighed. "But I want it all the time."

I chuckled. "We'll see."

"Hey!" McKenna said, her eyes looking past my shoulder.

Before I even glanced in that direction, I knew Rosie was approaching us. The skin on the back of my neck tingled. I forced myself to wait a beat before glancing over. As soon as my eyes landed on Rosie, my entire system felt jolted with a hot sizzle.

Her auburn hair was pulled up in a ponytail high on her head with loose tendrils dangling around her cheeks. Her skin was a little flushed, and my mind instantly conjured the memory of the freckles scattered all over her body, constellations that I'd teased with kisses.

Rosie's eyes met mine just as she stopped beside McKenna. She looked away quickly, fast enough that I couldn't read the expression there. McKenna swept her into a hug and began chattering about something before she looked my way. "Did you get your stitches out?" McKenna demanded.

"I already told you I did." I rolled my shoulder, reflexively checking to see how it felt. The incision felt sore, but that was about it. "I'm good to go."

McKenna pinned Rosie with her attention next. "Did you remove them and check it?"

Rosie's smile was bemused as she shook her head. "Wyatt must've had an appointment time when I wasn't there. Plus, the follow-ups aren't usually in the ER."

"Oh," my sister said, looking a little annoyed at this.

"We all know Rosie is the best nurse, but she can't do everything and be everywhere," my mother said.

McKenna pressed her lips together. "Fine. Don't do anything stupid like that again." She actually wagged her finger at me.

"It wasn't specifically my fault," I pointed out.

"It was Lia's," Blake said. "She's getting better, but when she cast her fishing line, it was a little too enthusiastic, and she caught Wyatt's shoulder."

There were a few chuckles around the group. "These things happen when you're learning to fish," I said.

I wanted to close the distance between Rosie and me, maybe ten feet, and kiss her. It appeared she'd come here from work. Her ponytail was a little lopsided on top, and she looked frazzled. For some women, the tendrils of hair dangling around their cheeks would've been a stylistic choice. Not so for Rosie. I loved that about her. She had a haphazard beauty.

Married or not, I knew it absolutely would not fly with her for me to kiss her here. Instead, I waited through what felt like endless casual conversation. In reality, it was maybe twenty minutes or so. Rosie broke away from the group finally, saying she had to go to the restroom. With everyone busy talking around us, there was enough distraction for me to think I might be able to catch her in the break room.

I discreetly talked my way out of a conversation with Blake and Griffin and wove my way around the perimeter of the room to slip into the back hallway. My timing couldn't have been better. Rosie was coming out of the bathroom at the back of the break room when I walked in. Only staff, family, and friends used this bathroom, so we had some privacy.

Pink flared on Rosie's cheeks when she saw me. She stepped back quickly. "Wyatt! What are you doing?" she hissed.

"We can either have this conversation out here or—"

She reached for my arm and yanked me in, tugging the door shut behind me. "Or here," I murmured. This was a wonderfully small bathroom, tiny even.

Rosie narrowed her eyes. "What?"

Her tone was demanding, and I wanted to tell her that it totally turned my crank, but I never wanted her to stop being bossy and demanding with me, so I wasn't about to tell her how much I loved it.

"Well, you're here," I pointed out.

As much as I wanted to touch her, and *holy hell*, I wanted to touch her, I didn't. It felt as if electricity shimmered around us with our own private electrical storm snapping and crackling. The sensation made me think of what I saw once after Mount Augustine had erupted near Anchorage when I was a little boy.

The plumes of volcanic ash had made these little clouds in some areas and the friction of the tiny particles rubbing together created sparks. It was like watching mini storms drift through the sky contained in their own burst of ash.

Rosie's cheeks flushed a deeper shade of pink, and her teeth snagged on her bottom lip. She reached up to tighten her ponytail. Her hands dropped, and she shifted on her feet. I sensed she was nervous, and protectiveness rose in a swift surge inside me.

All I wanted was to take care of her. Oh, I wanted far more than that, but the fierce need to protect and cherish her was different. I'd experienced plenty of chemistry in my life. Nothing came close to the chemistry I felt with Rosie, but the emotion twined within it amplified its power and depth.

Our gazes held while the air burgeoned with intensity as every second ticked by. As I studied her, I saw the vulnerability flickering in her gaze, a vulnerability I knew she tried to mask. My heart clenched tightly in my chest. I wanted Rosie on a bone-deep level. Yet I knew I had to be cautious to make sure I didn't push too far and too fast.

Maybe we were married. Okay, we *were* married.

But that was nothing more than a detail. Binding though it may be, to hold Rosie's heart, I had to be patient. Much as I wanted to let the fire take hold and spin us in its flames, I didn't. Not yet. I drew in a slow breath and kept a firm hold on my control.

"Can I kiss you?" I finally asked.

Chapter Eight

ROSIE

Can I kiss you?

Wyatt's question reverberated in the space between us.

It took me a minute, but the answer was a foregone conclusion as far as my body was concerned. I felt as if I were burning up inside. My knees were weak, and heat pooled in my belly as a tingling sensation radiated outward. I could barely breathe, and I was nearly desperate for air. Even more than air, I wanted the feel of his lips on mine.

I managed to draw in a shaky breath, unable to look away. All the while, I was anxious Wyatt could see all the fears that crowded my thoughts and heart and the vulnerability that I hated so much. I was so afraid he could see right through me. Even though I didn't want to admit it to myself, all of this was why I tried to ignore him after our fling a few years back.

And then, Vegas happened. Too long of trying to hold my feelings at bay and a chemistry so powerful it made me reckless.

Oh, how I wanted to play it cool with him!

Instead, one word betrayed me. "Please."

Just when I thought Wyatt might mock me and that there might be a tilt of a grin on his lips, he looked at me quietly, and his expression softened. He exuded a sense of protectiveness that helped me to feel safe, helped me to let go with him in a way that I couldn't with anyone else.

"Anything you want, sweetheart," he whispered.

My entire being felt as if it were arching toward him, near frantic for him. There wasn't much space in this bathroom, yet, the distance between us felt like a chasm.

The seconds ticked by. It couldn't have been maybe more than two or three seconds, yet, it felt like forever before he took a step closer. He lifted a hand and brushed one of the locks of my hair that had fallen loose away from my cheek. His finger brushed along the shell of my ear. Every subtle touch struck sparks that leaped over the surface of my skin and kindled the heat already burning inside higher and higher.

His fingers curled into a light fist, his knuckles brushing down along my neck before his hand unfurled again. He palmed my cheek, his thumb brushing over my bottom lip. My mouth parted. I could hardly breathe as my pulse pounded so hard I could hear the rush of it in my ears.

Once again, my voice betrayed all the secrets I wanted to keep. Well, one very specific secret — that I was desperate for him, that I wanted him so very, *very* much.

"Please, Wy—" His name was cut off, just as his lips brushed over mine.

I whimpered in relief. His kiss was all too brief, another brush of his lips, a tease with his tongue, and then he lifted his head. At the look in his eyes, my knees went weak.

"We're gonna need to get out of this bathroom," he said flatly.

"Oh!"

I was nearly shaking from the force of desire humming through my body. I had truly forgotten where we were. It was as if nothing existed outside this little bubble, this force field of electricity surrounding us.

I swallowed when Wyatt stepped back, and his hand dropped away from my cheek. "I'm gonna walk out. If there's anyone in the break room, I'll say something so you know, and you can lock the door. If you don't hear me say anything, give it a minute and then come out. I'll be in my office down the hallway in the brewery area. You've been back there before, right?"

I had to clear my throat to speak above a whisper. "Yes. But I don't know where your office is."

"When you go through the swinging doors into that area, it's the third door on the left. Just walk in. I'll be waiting."

Before I could say anything else, Wyatt had slipped out of the bathroom. I had to force myself to listen to hear if he spoke. When I didn't hear anything for a minute or so, I carefully opened the door and looked around. There wasn't a soul in sight, but I could hear the muted sounds from the crowded restaurant and the busy kitchen. The volume increased as I walked out of the break room into the hallway. I peered both ways. I felt as if I was committing some kind of crime.

I dashed down the hallway in the opposite direction from the restaurant and hurried through the swinging doors into the production area. Once the doors swung shut behind me, the sounds filtering down the hallway became much quieter. Adrenaline rushed through me, spinning like a storm within my desire.

I counted the doors as I dashed down the hall. My shoes actually squeaked on the tiled floor when I stopped in front of the third door. I was nearly out of breath as I reached for the handle. Before I could even touch it, the door opened, and Wyatt stood there. I hesitated for a beat, but then he reached for my hand and tugged me toward him. He closed the door behind us with his other hand. The sound of the lock clicking was loud.

I stared at him. His hand was warm around mine, his touch anchoring me inside. "This is your office," I said.

"It is."

Still out of breath, I took a moment to glance around. There wasn't a desk, but a large round table took up the back of the space. Neat stacks of papers occupied one side of it, and a notepad with a pencil rested atop it. Two chairs flanked it. Wyatt stepped backward, pulling me with him. Not that he had to pull hard. I would've gone anywhere with him.

I was still getting my bearings. In the other corner near the door was brewing equipment and a large whiteboard on the wall with notes written all over it.

"Should I take you on a tour?" Wyatt asked.

I finally brought my eyes back to his. I was instantly locked in his intense gaze.

I blinked and tried to collect myself mentally before giving up the fight. "Just kiss me. Please."

I thought he would kiss me, and I could forget all the worries and doubts tumbling in my mind, bouncing off each other and careening around like an out-of-control pinball machine.

"In a minute. I just need to ask you something." At my nod, he asked, "What do you want this to be?"

"What do you mean?"

"We're married. I think it's worth seeing if this can be something more than how we feel when we're together. I'm not even going to ask you how good it is when we kiss." Heat rose in my cheeks. My heart pounded along in a mad dash.

I couldn't lie to Wyatt and try to play it off. The moment we touched, I felt bracingly alive. Our connection was intense and fierce, underlaid with a passion I had never experienced before.

"I don't know," I answered honestly when I realized he was going to wait until I spoke. "I can't seem to bring myself to insist on some kind of divorce."

"Some kind of divorce? Is there more than one kind?" he asked lightly.

"You know what I mean. I'm just not sure what to do."

"We see how it goes. If you don't want anyone to know, then it's a little harder to see how it goes," he pointed out.

I managed to breathe. "I know. If everyone knows, they'll all have opinions, and I just want enough time to sort things out privately."

I thought he might argue the point on that, but he didn't. "I get it." He paused. At that moment, it felt like the air came alive, brimming with energy. His eyes darkened. "So right now I'm gonna bend you over and fuck you on that table. I'm also gonna take you home tonight and make sure you know that what we have is more than that."

Sweet hell. My knees nearly gave out. I felt a gush

of moisture between my thighs as I stared up at him. The idea of him bending me over and fucking me on that table was something I wanted so badly I could hardly bear the wait.

"After that, we see each other around town. Nobody will know we planned on seeing each other. We can have coffee together. See each other at locals' night. And maybe you'll let me come over and actually spend the night. Something like that."

His voice softened to a gruff rasp, and the look in his eyes sent my belly into a swoop. What he described was something we could maybe pull off. I wanted it so much I ached with it.

"What do you think about that?" he prompted.

I told the truth even though it made me vulnerable. "I'd like that," I whispered.

Wyatt's gaze turned molten. "To clarify, along with everything else, you would like me to bend you over and fuck you." His eyes flicked to the table immediately beside us.

I swallowed and shifted on my feet. I was so restless to relieve the ache in my very core. My breath was audible because I was that desperate. "Please. Hurry..."

In a fiery second, his mouth was on mine. His hands moved with knowledge and confidence. Wyatt knew my body. He knew how to kindle the need inside me higher and higher. There was something I loved about how he kind of manhandled me. He wasn't overpowering because that would've drawn up resistance in me. He simply took command, and I surrendered to what I knew he would give me.

He nipped the side of my neck, and I whimpered as I arched into him. He unbuttoned my blouse with nimble fingers, his thumb brushing across my nipples through my bra before he boldly sucked one into his mouth right through the silk. The sensation was sharp and piercing, and I cried out.

My hands were doing their own work, mapping his chest under his shirt, dragging over his cock through his jeans. "Hurry," I repeated.

I unbuttoned his jeans, and he shoved mine down around my hips before he turned me around to face the table. "Bend over, sweetheart."

I would've done anything this man asked. I bent over. The surface of the table was cool on my belly and breasts. My jeans were tight just above my knees, creating a sense of friction between my thighs. I cried out when his fingers delved into the core of me. I was already slippery wet for him, only for him. He murmured something before he withdrew his touch. I heard him say, "Oh, sweetheart."

A moment later, I heard the sound of a condom wrapper, and again, I said, "Hurry."

I couldn't even think when I was with Wyatt. It was all pure need driving me.

I felt the thick press of his crown at my entrance. "Are you sure?" he asked.

As if there was *any* question.

"Yes, please fuck me," I demanded.

I felt the press of his fingertips on one hip where he held me in place as he filled me in a swift thrust. I cried out, pressing back into the delicious stretch of him filling me.

His other palm slid up my back. I shimmied back again. "Please..."

His hand slid around my hip, and his fingers teased over my swollen clit as he pumped in and out of me in slow, rolling thrusts. I could hardly bear the friction of the motion with everything pressed tight as I bent over the table with my jeans banded around my knees.

Pleasure spun tighter and tighter, drawing deep to a point I could hardly bear. I heard myself saying his name, begging again. He finally created just a little more pressure over my clit. Sensation rose to a crescendo before it shattered inside me, and I was crying his name as the pleasure spun through me again and again.

I felt him tightening before I heard my name in a ragged cry. He shuddered over me before he curled around me and held me close. I felt sated, safe, and secure.

"I think I love you, Rosie," he whispered against my neck.

My heart thumped, crying out for me to voice my own feelings. I wasn't ready, so I simply breathed.

Chapter Nine

WYATT

Somehow, we disentangled ourselves and tugged our clothes halfway back on. With my remaining strength, I sat down on one of the chairs beside the table and pulled Rosie into my lap. She rested against me, her fingertips idly tracing along my collarbone just inside the vee of my shirt collar.

My heart was still pounding hard enough that it felt as if I had just run a sprint. She was soft and warm and I wanted to stay here in my office forever with her relaxed against me.

She eventually lifted her head, her eyes blinking a few times before she asked, "What now?"

I studied the sweet flush on her cheeks, the spray of freckles on her nose and cheeks, her kiss-swollen lips, and her gaze, startlingly unguarded. I wanted to ask her why she kept herself so buttoned up, but I knew the second I asked, she would get prickly. In a way, her prickliness was part of the attraction for me. Not because I wanted to fight it but because she was fierce and feisty, and I loved that about her. Every so often, like now, the knowledge that we had actually gotten married in Vegas would strike me and shock me a little. It was all so perfect and a cliché.

But I loved her and felt like I had lost the thread. Her fingers stilled on my collarbone before she thumped me lightly, right over my heart. "Did you hear me? What now?" she repeated.

My thoughts were a little sluggish, caught in the haze of desire. At her words, my pulse picked up its speed again. This was the hard part. When we were tangled up together, everything felt easy.

I had a short list of reasons I'd never been sure about relationships. Maybe it was bitterness. It all circled back to my family. We were a messy bunch, and things were better now, but our childhood had been difficult and painful. I'd seen what happened to my mom after our dad passed unexpectedly. She'd kind of fallen apart in her quiet, contained way. In the midst of her grief, she'd sort of checked out. When our grandfather rode roughshod over us, if she'd noticed, she hadn't had it in her to stop it.

And then, when Jake had lashed out at McKenna in his own wounded, broken way, it had just been one more dark lesson. It all came to a head the time I confronted him about it, and he drank himself to death the next night. Since I faced all of that, it just seemed easier to keep things at a distance when it came to emotions.

I'd always had a corner of me that wondered if I carried that capacity for my anger to drive me in the wrong direction. I liked to think that wasn't the case, but I didn't know.

Yet Rosie was my soft spot. I'd known years back that she was special, that she was worth the risk, and that maybe we could have it, *all* of it, ever after all.

Rosie brought my thoughts to this moment. "Wyatt?"

"We see how it goes. I think you're more worried about what others might think than I am."

She fidgeted a little on my lap and even that felt good. Vulnerability flickered in her eyes as she took a shaky breath. "It's not that I care what people think." Her fingers tapped lightly along my collarbone in a nervous gesture. I wanted to soothe her.

"I get it, Rosie." I leaned forward and kissed her quickly, drawing back before I lost myself in her again. "I think you don't want to feel pressured by what our friends might hope for. Is that it?"

She nodded, a tiny smile curling the corners of her lips and making me want to kiss her all over again.

"You know Griffin and I are living together right now."

"I know, and I figure he knows we're married."

I nodded slowly. "He does. Are you mad that I said something to him? It's hard to keep secrets from him."

"I know." She let out a soft sigh.

"I had to explain when he saw the wedding ring."

I wanted to tell her I loved her, but I knew she wasn't ready. I'd let it slip already tonight, but I hadn't meant to. I wasn't even sure she'd heard me. I was relieved she wasn't pissed off at me about Griffin knowing. It wasn't that I told him everything. But he'd guessed, and I couldn't deny it. I knew he'd know I was lying.

Rosie cleared her throat. "I'm staying in the small cabin on my dad's property. He's, uh, dealing with some health stuff. I need to be close, and he can't drive right now. But it's just me in the house. My brother stays in the main house with him."

"How's that going?" I asked, idly tracing circles on her knee.

She lifted one shoulder in a small shrug. "It's okay."

We'd both grown up in Fireweed Harbor, so I knew her family. Her dad had owned the small hardware shop in town since I was a kid. I knew her mom had died when her brother was a baby, but I didn't know many other details.

When she didn't offer more, I focused on her earlier comment. "Are you telling me all this because I can come to your house?" My lips tugged at the corners.

Her cheeks went a little pink. She pressed her lips together, trying not to smile, but then she gave in and giggled. I wanted to kiss her all over again.

"Yes."

"Does that mean I can come over tonight?" I asked, my voice low.

"Tonight?" she squeaked.

"Yes. I want to sleep beside you, sweetheart."

Her lashes swept down, and she tapped her fingers along my collarbone again. "Okay."

"Are you working tomorrow?"

Her lashes lifted, and she nodded. "I have to leave for work at seven. I usually go get coffee in town."

"Perfect. I'll meet you there. We're going to drive separately to meet and have coffee."

"After you spend the night at my house?" she asked.

"Yup. I'll run into you at the coffee shop, and no one will know we just had a whole night together."

"Wyatt—"

I cut her off with a quick kiss. "Rosie, you know how good it was for us that week. You know how good it was just tonight. No sense in going to all the trouble of getting a divorce if maybe it's worth it."

She studied me. "Are you serious, Wyatt?" she finally asked.

I held her gaze, wondering just how much to say. I decided to toe the edge of the truth without going too far into it. "Yes. It's never been this good for me with anyone. I think that might be the case for you. Why not see if we can have more?"

She stayed quiet, vulnerability flickering in her eyes. I wanted to hold her close and make sure she knew her heart was safe with me. Yet I knew she wasn't quite there yet and pushing too far too fast would blow up.

"I already know you, and you already know me. What if it's even better?" I added.

A few days later

"Dad, I got it," I said as I walked into the garage, where he was trying to heft something onto the top of a metal shelf.

My dad let out a grunt of frustration as he turned to face me and lowered his arms. "I should be able to do this."

I glanced down to see that the wheels on the metal shelving weren't locked into place. Leaning over, I quickly clicked the locks on the caster wheels before straightening. "Now you can," I replied with a reassuring smile.

My dad chuckled. "I kept wondering why the shelf kept moving. Wasn't thinking." He quickly reached up and placed his box of fishing gear precisely where he wanted it on the top shelf, where it had been stored for as long as I could remember.

"Fishing lately?" I asked as we turned together and

walked toward the door that led into the kitchen from the garage.

"Just went yesterday."

"You did?"

My dad waggled his brows as he held the door open for me as I walked through. "You don't know everything I do, Rosie."

I rolled my eyes as I sat down in the chair by the kitchen table. "I don't want to know everything you do, Dad."

"Would you like some coffee?" he asked.

I shook my head. "Thank you, but no. I'm headed in to meet Tessa and McKenna for coffee before work."

"Excellent. I'd ask for a ride, but Derek is picking me up."

"I love that you and Derek are friends," I said.

"Well, I'm the old wise one in our friendship," he teased. His gaze sobered. "Pretty soon, though, Derek's going to be all better. He's not gonna want to hang with an old guy like me."

I cocked my head to the side. "I'm fairly confident you'll still see plenty of Derek. Maybe you got to know each other because you both hang around at the hospital together, but you're pretty awesome. Plus, you know all the best fishing spots."

My dad flashed me a grin as he sat down across from me and took a swallow of his coffee. "I know. I'm just teasing. Derek is a good egg. If your brother doesn't wanna run the hardware store, and Derek's feeling up to it, I might hire him when I'm ready to be done."

"Speaking of Brent, where is he?"

My father's eyes arced up to the clock mounted on

the wall above the kitchen stove. "I don't know. He's not an early riser like you. Never has been."

"Well, everyone has their own circadian rhythm," I offered. I tried to ignore the worry that danced along the edges of my thoughts.

I didn't like thinking about it, but I still sensed something was afoot with my brother. I had no idea what or what to even do about it, even if I knew. I also knew that it grated on my brother that I worried about him so much. That was the downside to being the older sister with almost eight years between us. I babysat for him a lot when we were growing up.

I shoved the worries away as soon as my brother's voice came from behind me.

"My circadian rhythm is shifting," Brent announced with a jaunty grin. He gave my father a squeeze on the shoulder as he walked by. "I have to get to work."

"How is that going?" I asked, doing my very best to keep my voice casually curious.

He glanced over as he poured himself a cup of coffee. "It's actually going great. I enjoy working with Kenan, and it's never boring."

The constant tension between my shoulder blades eased a tiny bit. My brother sounded legitimately motivated.

"Good to hear," I replied.

My dad took a swallow of his coffee as he looked over at my brother. "He's been saying this every morning since he started at Fireweed Industries."

"What exactly do you do?" I asked as Brent sat in the remaining chair at the small round kitchen table.

"It's different every day, which is why I love it. The other day, we helped unload equipment for the brewery. Some days, we do stuff at the warehouse, where they keep all the vehicles for road maintenance. Sometimes, we're at the headquarters doing odd jobs. I show up, and Kenan either takes me along with him or sends me somewhere else to do something. It's awesome."

My dad's gaze held pride as he looked over at my brother. "That's a good place to get your foot in the door. Fireweed Industries is a big deal."

Worry was like a vine tangled in my thoughts when it came to my brother. College had been hard for him. He'd partied hard and then dropped out. All things considered, it seemed like the best thing because otherwise, it was like tossing money into the wind to pay for it.

"I know," Brent said. "I'm not under any illusions. It's a big business, but it's a family business. I like it and the pay is pretty good."

Just then, my phone vibrated in my pocket. I slipped it out of my pocket and glanced at the screen. "Oh! I need to get going. I forgot I need to meet McKenna because she's dropping her car off at the mechanic's shop. Jack is out at a fire."

I gave my dad a kiss on the cheek and waved to both of them before hurrying out the door. A short drive later, I slowed to a stop in front of McKenna's driveway. She waited in her car at the end, as planned. She pulled out in front of me, and I followed her into town to the local garage.

A few minutes later, she hopped in my passenger seat. "Hey! Thanks for picking me up."

"Of course," I replied. "When will Jack be back?" Her hotshot firefighter husband was out of town dealing with a fire somewhere in the wilderness.

"Next week," she said.

I smiled over at her. "You miss him?"

"Of course, I do. And it feels ridiculous. I mean—" She let out a quick sigh. "I'm used to being on my own."

"But you're in love," I teased as I slowed to turn into the parking lot beside Spill the Beans Café."

McKenna laughed softly. "True story. Who knew?"

"Everyone but you as soon as we saw you with him," I replied.

My thoughts spun to Wyatt. I couldn't help but wonder if anybody had similar thoughts when they saw us together. The intensity of my reaction to him when we happened to be in each other's vicinity was startlingly powerful. I kept thinking it would dissipate

McKenna and I walked in together, hopping into the back of the line. As if the universe knew I was thinking about Wyatt, the café door opened a moment later with the friendly bell chiming. Before I even glanced in the direction of the door, my body knew Wyatt had just entered the café. Goose bumps rose on the back of my neck with a little jolt of electricity zipping through my body.

I told myself I was imagining things, but then McKenna exclaimed, "Griffin! Wyatt!"

I could totally play it cool. No one needed to know what was going on with Wyatt and me. But then, I wondered why I wanted to keep it a secret. I worried that everyone would have an opinion, and if it didn't work out, everyone would also have an opinion about that. Maybe not everyone, but certainly our friends, most of whom were mutual.

And when he breaks your heart, how will you keep that a secret?

Even though I didn't like to think about it, I knew why I let things die on the vine back when we had our week-long fling. I hadn't even had to avoid him then because he went his way, and I went mine. He hadn't been living here in Fireweed Harbor, so there was nothing to avoid. Much as I tried to pretend it hadn't been *that* good with him, that was such a lie. That week had been insanely hot. All this time, I'd tried to convince myself it had been a fluke.

No one had measured up since then, not even close. Although it would've been easier if it was just the burning-hot chemistry, I knew it wasn't. I didn't want to be hopeful, but my heart sure did. Little drumbeats of hope and wishfulness got loud every time I let myself think too much about Wyatt.

You don't know if it's going to work out. You have perfectly good reasons for being careful.

Careful. That was what I told myself it was. I'd been old enough to have a fairly vivid memory of what it had been like when my mother had died unexpectedly. She'd gone to the hospital to give birth to my little brother and never come home. What was supposed to be a joyful event had been devastating. The grief had been a shock of such force, I'd felt knocked flat and hadn't really known how to process any of it.

I'd also witnessed what it did to my father. He had been utterly distraught and trying to hold it together for me and his new baby boy.

My mother had spiraled into a medical condition called disseminated intravascular coagulation (DIC) after she gave birth. I only knew this because I came across my mother's medical records when my father asked for help shredding old tax documents. He must've forgotten they were there. I'd been in nursing school at the time and asked one of the OB-GYNs on staff about it. DIC wasn't specific to childbirth. In short, it was when all the complicated steps involved in blood clotting went haywire. Blood could clot where it wasn't supposed to and run freely where it should be clotting. It could be triggered after major physical trauma of any kind, infection, and more. Women with childbirth complications were at risk of DIC, and it could rapidly become a dire medical situation.

In the medical world, there was a phrase: *All bleeding stops*. Either a person's blood clots properly or a person lost enough blood to die. In all cases, the bleeding stopped. Modern medicine was not magic. If a person's blood wasn't clotting properly, medical professionals could only do so much to save them. My mother had faced something that even the best hospitals and doctors in the world could only pray to stop. No medical professional wanted to consider it, but in some cases, it could truly boil down to luck if someone pulled through. My mother wasn't lucky that day.

She'd been able to hold my brother while she'd been dying, and I could only wonder what that must've been like for her. I was terrified that the same thing might happen to me. Even though I knew the chances were slim, and it was one of those fluke situations.

All this to say, I didn't want to be distraught if I lost someone the way my father had. I was afraid to have a child. Statistically speaking, the odds were in my favor, but then we tended to forget just how dangerous having a baby could be in the modern era.

"Are you okay?" Tessa's voice broke through my train of thought.

I glanced toward her. "Oh, yeah," I said quickly.

I didn't even know why my thoughts had detoured. That train of thought was a dead-end road I got stuck in sometimes, one where I couldn't change anything that happened.

Wyatt was at the counter with Griffin, and McKenna was talking with him about something. I could feel Tessa's gaze on me still. I glanced back in her direction. "What?" My tone was defensive.

Tessa's brows hitched up slightly. "What's with you and Wyatt?"

"What do you mean?"

She pressed her lips together to keep from smiling but then gave up, shrugging with a little grin. "Just that, it's kind of obvious you two..."

"We what?" I willed the heat to dissipate from my cheeks to no avail because my face was on fire.

"You look at him a lot, he looks at you a lot, and it's obvious you might like each other."

The look on my face must've given away my distress. Tessa took pity on me. "If it helps, I under-stand why you might not want to do anything about it or want to talk about it. I mean, if you are doing anything about it, or thinking about doing anything about it," Tessa clarified when my eyes widened in alarm. "That's how I felt when things started with Adam and me. We all share the same friends. And even if we didn't, this is a small town. Gossip is a real thing. If you're hoping to keep things private, or see how they go, or get your heart broken privately—" Tessa cut off sharply.

I knew I must've looked horrified or maybe already distraught. She reached over and squeezed my hand across the table quickly. "Wyatt is not going to break your heart."

I forced myself to breathe slowly. "How do you know?"

Tessa wasn't one to gossip, so I decided to let down my guard a little.

"Because he's a nice guy. I don't know what's going on, and I'm certainly not expecting you to tell me now or even later. But the whole family shares the same baggage. You know it. Everybody deals with things differently, and I'm not sure how Wyatt has dealt with it. But I know he's a good man. Remember, he's the one who helped McKenna be open about what happened to her with Jake."

All I could do was take in what she was saying because, at that moment, I heard McKenna's voice behind us.

Tessa's voice was low when she added, "We can talk anytime."

The next few moments were a jumble as people pulled extra chairs up to the table. The next thing I knew, Wyatt was sitting down beside me. Griffin happened to take the chair across from me. With my awareness that he knew about Wyatt and me, I tried not to look at him too much, or I'd get more self-conscious than I already felt.

This wasn't the first time I had wondered why it was just Wyatt who drew me to him. Every man in that family was graced with good looks. They were certainly charmed when it came to what nature bestowed. When I looked at Griffin, it was with an objective appreciation. Not one single spark fired inside me, and my pulse beat at a regular speed.

But the second I even thought about looking at Wyatt, along with merely having him seated beside me, my pulse kicked along faster and faster.

Relieved by the distraction of conversation with others, I was able to wrangle my pulse at least sort of under control and felt proud of myself. I could handle being with Wyatt in public.

Until I felt his palm slide onto my thigh, his touch warm and sure. I was caught between two competing impulses — the urge to brush his palm away to get my hormones to chill out and the urge to savor his touch. I loved it so *very* much when he touched me.

"How are you doing, Rosie?" Wyatt's voice was low and rumbly.

Chapter Eleven

WYATT

"I'm fine," Rosie squeaked.

She placed her hand over mine, where it rested on her thigh, and I could feel the tension in her touch. For a moment, I thought she would brush my hand away, but then she laced her fingers in mine and squeezed.

"How are you?" she asked.

I could tell she was a little nervous by the sound of her voice. It was an octave higher than usual.

She took a swallow of her coffee and shifted in her seat before she looked up at me. Her cheeks were a little pink, and I wanted to kiss her. Story of my life.

When I'd sat down a moment ago and decided to tease her a little, I thought I had things under control. But Rosie took my control and snapped it into pieces. I was faltering, stumbling, reaching to get ahold of myself.

Griffin asked me something, but I didn't even notice until he prompted, "Wyatt? Losing your hearing over there?"

"Excuse me? I was zoning out," I hedged.

As soon as I met my brother's eyes, I knew that he was giving me shit because I was distracted by Rosie. I didn't care. He started talking to me about something to do with whether I would sub in on the fire crew in town.

Just when I thought I'd been able to get myself focused, Rosie unlaced her fingers from mine and placed her hand on my cock. I wore jeans, so it was tight down there. I gritted my teeth and felt the swell of it when she boldly stroked up and down.

"So I thought you were done with firefighting?" she asked, her tone all innocent.

I cleared my throat. "I am," I gritted out. "But if they need help, I can sub in for local things."

Another stroke of her palm over my length, and I now deeply regretted teasing her.

Maybe Griffin didn't know exactly what was happening, but when I caught my brother's eyes again, he simply shook his head before he glanced at Rosie and winked. "Sometimes Wyatt has trouble paying attention. Have you ever noticed that?"

————

"You just wait. I'll get you back."

Griffin chuckled as he hooked his hand around the back of a chair and spun it around to sit down. He straddled the chair and rested his elbows on the back. "Maybe? But I'd have to be susceptible."

"Susceptible?"

"You're gaga over Rosie. I'm not gaga over anybody."

I narrowed my eyes at him. "Well, when you're a little older, you might be."

I was a whole fifteen minutes older than Griffin. I didn't really care, nor did he, but it was a source of rank when I wanted to use it.

Griffin rolled his eyes, but he didn't take the bait. "In all seriousness, what the hell *is* going on with you and Rosie? Aside from the fact that you're married. Minor detail, but the devil's in the details."

"Who's married?" Our sister's voice came through the door ahead of her.

I narrowed my eyes at Griffin.

"Wyatt. He's married to his job," Griffin said quickly. "He worked like a dog when he was a fire-fighter. As far as I can tell, he's working too many hours now that he took over handling all the brewing stuff." Griffin's gaze swung back toward me. "You should take this up with HR."

I burst out laughing, and McKenna narrowed her eyes. "No one is making Wyatt work too much."

"I love my job," I assured McKenna. "I'm not the only one who works a lot. The worst culprit is Rhys when it comes to working long hours."

McKenna let out a little sigh. "I know. He's been better since they had Jake, but still," she said, referring to our nephew.

"Want me to take him to task about that?" Griffin teased.

"I already do."

"She does," Rhys said, joining the conversation as he walked through the door.

"What is this? Family afternoon in the brewing area?" I joked.

Rhys rested his hips against the stainless-steel table where I had been jotting down notes on a notepad for some tweaks I made with the brewing recipes. He flashed me a grin. "Sure. Should we have a family afternoon in the brewing area every week? I'm all in." His gaze sobered before he pushed away from the table and pulled me into a backslapping hug. "I'm just glad you're here. I thought I'd come over here and do a loop around."

Blake walked into the room while Rhys was talking and waggled his brows when he caught my eyes. "Told you."

"Told me what?" I prompted.

"It'd be good for you to be here. We need you."

Just when I was about to reply, Adam strolled in with Kenan.

"It's legit a family meeting," Kenan quipped.

Ever since I moved home, I'd wondered if I should've come home sooner. I could easily dismiss my reasons for being away from Fireweed Harbor, the place that was home to me in my heart and soul, the only place where I felt like I really belonged. Yet, as I glanced around at my siblings, I knew that I needed to be away. That time had given me the perspective necessary to find peace.

Rhys and Blake joked about something while McKenna was talking about public relations plan she had to help with, of all things, the finance department. "To make finance fun," she said.

When my eyes landed on Rhys again, and he smiled over at me, a tightness I'd been carrying in my chest eased a little more. Jake had chronologically been our oldest brother, and for as long as I could remember, my first memories of him were of him being mean. McKenna was the youngest, the last one behind Griffin and me, and she had been his main target. Even when I was younger, I'd felt like I was supposed to look up to Jake, but I never had. Rhys had been and still was the older brother who I looked to for everything.

He'd come through once again. When McKenna was finally honest with the family about how Jake had targeted her verbally and sometimes physically, just brutal at times, he'd never questioned her and supported her completely. When I was a little boy, so much smaller than Jake, I felt as if I had failed her. Both of us had found some solace in sharing the truth and how the family responded.

There'd been a few hiccups, but then recognizing someone you loved, who had been through something horrible, could also do hurtful things was a painful kernel of knowledge to accept. Jake drinking himself to death in college made perfect sense when I considered all he wanted to forget.

Rhys's reaction to the abuse in our family had been the opposite of Jake's. He eschewed any aggression and was careful to manage his emotions. I suppose it had been the opposite for all of us. We were all protective of those we loved. Rhys hadn't hesitated when he heard what McKenna had experienced at Jake's hands. He instantly believed her, which had been healing for her and me. Griffin had also known, but I think it felt more like a secondary secret for him. He kept it quiet because I'd asked him to. I would've done the same for him.

He was still keeping my last secret. I still felt that weight on me, but I didn't know if it was worth putting out there.

"You okay?" I hadn't even noticed Griffin had come to stand beside me.

I met his gaze as I nodded. "I am." It didn't take much for us to communicate. I wasn't sure if it counted as mind reading, but he knew that I had just been thinking about that last secret.

I didn't want to dwell on it, so I shifted focus. "Good catch back there with McKenna."

Griffin chuckled. "You *do* work too much, but I wouldn't describe you as married to your job."

———

Many hours later, I eyed my phone. Before I began to dwell for too long, I spun it around, lifting it and tapping out a text.

Me: *Can I see you tonight?*

My heart kicked faster, beating a reverberating drumroll in my chest as I waited to see if and when Rosie might reply.

One of the things I loved about her—I truly did love her, even if I knew she wasn't ready for it yet — was that she wasn't one for playing games. She wouldn't leave me on read, and she wouldn't delay a response. She would respond when she could, and if there was a delay, it was because she was busy.

I was lucky this night. I only had to wait seven minutes. Not that I was counting.

Rosie: *I'm just finishing up a shift at the hospital. I'll be heading home in about 15 minutes. Where should I meet you?*

Me: *Your place or mine? Your call.*

I watched as the dots appeared and smiled to myself. I could literally feel the wheels of her brain turning as she weighed the pros and cons of the options.

Rosie: *My place. 20 minutes.*

Me: *I thought you said 15?*

Rosie: *Sigh. I'm leaving here in 15 minutes and have to drive home.*

Me: *That's five extra minutes I have to wait. Forgive me for my impatience.* 😉

Rosie: *Forgiven.*

What I typed next was impulsive, but I didn't regret it.

Chapter Twelve

ROSIE

Wyatt: *For the record, I'm in love with you.*

"Ohmygodohmygodohmygodohmygod!"

Fortunately, I was the only person in my car to hear myself. I was freaking the hell out.

I hadn't forgotten that Wyatt had whispered that he'd loved me in the heat of the moment. My little heart desperately wanted it to be true, but I could chalk that up to being overcome by lust. Maybe. Or if I could scrounge up the courage, I could admit I was all up in my feels when it came to Wyatt.

I had to force myself to actually breathe. I felt a little lightheaded from the lack of oxygen. Denial was a safe space, at least when it came to feelings. When I got some oxygen to my brain, I contemplated Wyatt and feelings and me, and why I always shied away from letting myself think too deeply about anyone.

I remember when I was in high school, and I had this crush on a boy. My dad had sat me down and told me I would have crushes on people and not to be afraid. He'd told me that the expression *"it was better to have loved and lost than to have never loved at all"* was something he believed deeply. He'd said he missed my mom but would never regret loving her.

The little girl in me who hadn't known what to do when my mom was just gone one day, especially after a day that was supposed to be so exciting, had been extremely skeptical about this. Dad had come home with my baby brother, and I'd never seen my mother again. I knew now, in the clear light of adulthood and as an ER nurse, that the medical team had valiantly tried to keep her alive. Yet once what started in her happened, it was like a ball rolling down a hill. There were no brakes to stop it. The medical team would've thrown one thing after another in the way, hoping and praying she'd somehow pull through. In the end, none of those things could staunch the bleeding.

I was scared of caring too much for anyone. I was terrified to fall in love. I was afraid to have anyone matter that much. My father had seemed desolate in the aftermath of my mother's death, but he'd pulled himself together. I'd been a little girl who hadn't known how to absorb the shock of it and the after-shocks that still rippled through my life from that loss.

I was also afraid to think seriously about the idea of commitment and family because I loved babies. I wanted a family, but I was utterly terrified to have a baby. I didn't even know how to have a conversation with someone about the depth of my fear. It felt like a chasm I couldn't cross.

I'd seen a therapist when I was a little girl and then again after I started nursing school and came to an understanding of what had actually happened to my mother. I recalled the therapist pointing out that my job illuminated something that could maybe help ease my fear. That life was truly random, and so many other things could happen. Intellectually, I understood that, but the emotional little girl inside me who'd lost her mom was still so very frightened.

Having Wyatt just lay his feelings out there blew my mind. I also recognized the courage it took for him to do that. Beyond the gossip circulating about the Cannon family, the family could be seen as lucky because they had so much wealth. Yet they shared a tangled and painful history. It was all very messy, and I had been McKenna's friend through most of it. My home had been a safe place for her.

Wyatt was boldly and courageously putting his heart right out there for me, and I was terrified. I'd known nothing but love growing up. My father was the best father I could imagine, somehow pulling himself together and doing the best he could to take care of me and Brent when we were growing up. Even though the pain of my mother's loss was still a sharp ache, my only memories of her were loving and warm.

Wyatt's text bounced around in my thoughts as I drove home from work. When I got home, I glanced at the clock on my dashboard. Wyatt would probably be here in a few minutes. My eyes arced through the trees toward the main house. My brother's car wasn't there. My worry was like a reflex when it came to him.

Shoving those worries away, I turned off my car. I climbed out and rounded to the passenger side to get my backpack and purse. Just as I was closing the door, a pair of headlights illuminated me. I glanced toward the head of the driveway to recognize the shape of Wyatt's truck. There were plenty of trucks in Fireweed Harbor, yet I knew this one belonged to Wyatt. My heart began pounding hard and fast in my chest.

I waited because it seemed silly to rush inside. A moment later, he had parked beside my car and climbed out. I had taken a step back and could feel the cool metal of my car behind me.

"Hey, Rosie," Wyatt said, his voice a little rumbly.

I had to clear my throat to even speak. Heat buffeted me like the rush of a fire when the wind blew. "Hey!" I squeaked.

I hadn't remembered to leave on my porch light, so we had nothing but the silvery light from the moon shining above. It was maybe three-quarters full and cast Wyatt's face half in shadow. His features were etched in the pearly light—the angled line of a cheekbone, the sharp cut of his jaw, his wide full lips, and his eyes caught in the light, starlight blue, almost brighter for the contrast with the darkness.

He took a step closer. Even though it felt impossible, my pulse began to race faster and faster.

I couldn't think at all when he asked, "How are you?"

My fingers tightened around the handle of my backpack. I clutched my backpack and purse with both hands, and they dangled in front of my knees.

"Rosie?" he prompted.

My brain caught up to the conversation like a rubber band snapping back into place. "I'm fine. Busy day. It's always busy at the hospital."

I felt a little lightheaded again, almost dizzy from his presence.

"Can I get your bags?" he asked.

I nodded as he reached for them and felt his fingers brush against mine. His touch was a jolt of fiery electricity that raced up my arm and swirled into the heat spinning inside me.

He stepped closer, lifting his other hand and catching one of the loose tendrils of my hair dangling down around my neck where it had fallen loose from my ponytail. He twirled it around his fingers. When I felt the brush of his knuckles against my neck, I practically arched up into his touch like a cat purring.

"Um, how was your day?" I belatedly asked.

"Busy. A different kind of busy than you deal with at the hospital." He paused, his thumb brushing along the edge of my jaw and up across my bottom lip. My mouth parted, and I felt the slick heat between my thighs when my channel clenched at nothing more than his touch.

He took another step closer, his body coming flush against mine. With his heat in front of me and the metal of the car behind me, my nerves felt alive and shimmering from the contrast.

"Can I kiss you, Rosie?" he rasped.

With my heartbeat pounding and my breath shallow, I sucked in a quick breath. I was still teetering on the edge of being woozy from his mere presence, but I managed to nod.

Wyatt took another step closer. When one of his arms slid around my waist and his palm flattened in the center of my back, his presence soothed the wildness in me. It didn't make sense. My need was so fierce, such a rush. It was like water tumbling over the edge of a cliff, the velocity accelerating out of control. Yet his presence caught me in that tumbling surge. I could feel the heat of his palm on my back, his touch anchoring me in the moment.

He lifted his other hand, palming my cheek. His thumb traced along the edge of my jaw, curving up to slide another slow brush across my bottom lip. I was caught in the beam of his heated gaze. Time felt slow and fast at once.

I didn't realize I was holding my breath until he dipped his head and his lips brushed over mine. My breath released in a soft, needy sigh. Finally, *finally*, he fit his mouth over mine and kissed me.

I loved the way Wyatt kissed me, gentle and commanding. He always started slow. It felt as if he were kindling the flames rising higher and higher inside me. With lingering brushes of his lips over mine, a kiss dropped at one corner of my mouth and then the other. Heat pooled low in my belly, air rushing into the fire and building its heat rapidly.

His tongue swept into my mouth with little teases at first until I let out an impatient sound in the back of my throat. He shifted incrementally closer, bringing the full force of his strength and warmth against my body. His hand slid down my back to curve over my bottom. With a subtle pressure from his touch, I felt the hot length of his arousal nestled in the cradle of my hips.

He angled his head to the side, taking control of our kiss. Deep sweeps of his tongue against mine shifted from slow to messy and devouring. I couldn't get enough of him. I was gasping, and our teeth clinked together. He was rocking, nudging his hips into mine, and I could feel the slippery heat of my arousal, my panties drenched with it.

Wyatt lifted his head, and we stared at each other. The moonlight above offered a shimmery light. An owl hooted in the trees, and another one answered from a distance. Seconds later, its wings softly whooshed through the air above us.

I shifted on my feet, restless and nearly aching with need. Even though I could feel the cool air on my skin and hear the sounds of the breeze rustling through the trees and the call of another bird somewhere in the darkness nearby, I forgot where we were.

Everything narrowed to Wyatt, to the feel of his hard, muscled body pressing against mine.

The cotton scrubs I had on were thin and loose. When I moved again, my hips instinctively arched toward him. His hand slid down my side, his thumb brushing across the tight peak of one of my nipples.

His gaze never broke from mine. He shifted back incrementally, just enough for him to slide his hand under the hem of my shirt and behind the not-sexy-at-all scrubs. There was no preliminary teasing. His fingers dipped right down into my cotton panties, sliding into my slippery wet folds. I bit my lip, crying out when he grazed the flat of his fingers over my clit where it was pressed outward, swollen and needy.

Wyatt's eyes were dark on mine. My lips were parted as I stared back at him. His fingers slid deeper into me. I moved my feet apart, just enough for him to sink two fingers inside. The friction created by me standing while he pumped his fingers into me was beyond intoxicating. My orgasm was already waiting. I was toeing the edge of pleasure coming in sharp little bursts as he pumped his fingers in and out. "Sweetheart, you feel so good," he whispered against my cheek.

"Wyatt..." I pleaded on a ragged breath.

My hips rocked up into his touch. His fingers stroked deeply, stretching me. With the heel of his hand sliding over my clit, I toppled over the edge. I cried out, my shoulder blades pressing against my car. I felt his thumb teasing over my clit, pushing the orgasm and the pleasure higher and higher as I shuddered against the car, one of my palms slapping against the side.

Without the car and one of his arms around my waist to hold me steady, I was certain I would've collapsed. My knees were wobbly and weak. All of me was shaking and trembling as the pleasure broke through me in rippling waves.

My climax eventually slowed, and he drew his hand out, making sure to tuck my panties into place and tighten the drawstring on my waistband. Just when I thought I couldn't be any more aroused, he lifted his hand and licked my arousal off his fingers. His eyes held mine the entire time. I could hardly breathe as I stared at him. My heart was pounding with a sweet tightening just above my belly.

My awareness sharpened, and I heard the breeze rustling in the trees again as I realized Wyatt had just fucked me with his fingers against my car just outside my house. I never lost control like this. *Never*. It belatedly occurred to me that I should be grateful his truck shielded us from the view from my father's house.

I distantly heard the sound of tires on gravel and realized my brother must've just turned into the driveway. I took an unsteady breath.

"We need to go in," I whispered.

As I stepped away from my car and Wyatt reached for my hand, I heard my breath still coming in ragged gasps and the distant sound of an owl calling, followed by another. I was hot, through and through, and savored the cool night air on my cheeks.

Chapter Thirteen

WYATT

It was a miracle I could even walk. My knees were shaky, and my entire body felt drawn tight with arousal. My swollen cock pressed painfully against my zipper.

Holding tight to Rosie's hand, I walked with her to her door. My need was pounding through me in a rolling beat that kept racing faster and faster. My mind was hazed, and I clung to strands of control threatening to break.

All I could think was, *Rosie. More.*

We stumbled through the door, and I'd barely gotten it closed behind me when she turned. Her eyes were dark, her hair falling loose from its lopsided ponytail. For the first time since I'd arrived, I took her in. Everything before this had been pure sensation.

She wore a pair of green scrubs with a jacket hanging half open. She didn't have a lick of makeup on. Her cheeks were flushed and her eyes a deep green. It felt like staring into a forest.

I wasn't really thinking when her palm landed on my chest, and she pushed me back against the door.

Knocked off balance, I stumbled slightly before my shoulders collided with the door.

I opened my mouth to say something just as she said, "Your turn."

The sly, teasing glint in her eyes sent a shot of blood to my aching cock. Her palm slid down my chest and over my abs. I distantly heard her keys falling to the floor, followed by a thump, which had to be her purse. Next thing I knew, her hands made quick work of the button, and zipper on my jeans. She moved boldly as her hand slid straight into my boxer briefs and curled around my length. She stroked me once, her eyes on mine. She bit her bottom lip, her lips curling into a small smile. I felt her thumb slide across my cock, swiping the come that was already rolling out.

I sucked in a deep breath, nearly desperate for air. "Rosie —" I bit out.

"Anything you want." She shoved my jeans down a little bit around my hips, still holding my cock as she freed it. "After I do this," she added as she leaned over and licked the tip of my cock, making a satisfied little hum in her throat.

My palm slapped against the door. Whatever I meant to say next became indecipherable with the low, ragged groan I let out. My head thumped against the door behind me when she sucked me into her mouth. My attention narrowed to the sensation of her teasing tongue gliding along the underside of my cock, the suction when she drew me deeply in her mouth, and the sound of the pop when she released me before sucking me in again.

"Fuck," I growled as I laced my fingers in her hair and held on while she proceeded to drive me closer and closer to the edge.

When I said her name, I was distantly shocked at my pleading. I didn't usually beg. But right now, I needed her to topple me over the edge. I needed the sweet relief.

She made that little humming sound in her throat in response as she sucked me in deep. That was enough. My climax rushed through me in a piercing jolt. I cried out, my release spurting into her mouth.

I was grateful for the door behind me. Without it, I doubted I would still be standing. Rosie slowly rocked back on her heels. After the force of my climax, the way she tucked me back in and buttoned my jeans gently was a stark contrast.

By the time I had gathered myself enough to think, she had stood and was leaning over to fetch her keys and purse off the floor before setting them on a small table beside her door.

She looked over at me. I already knew I loved her, but at that moment, it felt as if the emotions and intimacy between us were a living, breathing force. She lifted her chin a little. I felt like it was a small gift, but she didn't break eye contact. I could feel her vulnerability rippling just under the surface. She was so strong on the outside. Yet I knew the core that lay underneath was all the stronger for her vulnerability. It was that vulnerability I wanted to protect, to cradle close, and to cherish.

A growling stomach—not mine—snapped through the moment. Rosie rolled her eyes. "I'm starving. I usually forget to eat at work."

"I bet you do," I said softly.

She stepped back, a small smile teasing the corners of her lips. "You don't need to tell me that I should make sure to eat at work. I know I should."

"I wouldn't dream of pointing that out." My tone was dry.

"Are you hungry?" she tossed that question over her shoulder when she turned and began walking from the small living room area toward the kitchen.

My gaze circled about her place. I'd been in here before, but I hadn't taken the time to look around. I knew her father had rented this place out for many years. This small place was just about perfect for one or two people. Although it was dark outside now, I knew the living room windows were oriented to face toward the harbor. There was an efficiency propane stove in the corner with a comfortable-looking couch and an ottoman facing the television mounted on the wall.

The kitchen to the other side was small and cute with an arched window and a small built-in dining booth tucked into the corner. Opposite the kitchen were three doors, one which I knew led to Rosie's bedroom and bathroom. A small half-bathroom was off the living room and what I presumed was another bedroom to the side.

"Wyatt?" Rosie prompted.

My mind caught up to her question. "I have eaten, but I can always eat more." I glanced at my watch. "It's late, though. Please don't tell me you're going to offer to cook me something. That's not necessary," I said as I followed her lead and kicked off my boots in the shoe tray near the door.

She grinned. "I'm too tired to cook. I have one of those frozen pizzas that I could make. Or is that beneath you?" She waggled her brows as she stood in front of the freezer.

"I'm a guy. Frozen pizza is not above me. When I was firefighting, I lived off freeze-dried food."

"Yeah, but your family has a really good restaurant, and they make kick-ass pizza."

"Well, let's order some. It'll probably be here by the time your frozen pizza cooks," I pointed out. I was already sliding my phone out of my pocket and lifting it to make a call.

"Wyatt, you don't have to do that," Rosie began.

As the phone rang in my ear, I caught her eyes. "It's pizza, Rosie. Just pizza. The delivery guy isn't going to spread any rumors."

"What if—"

Before I could respond, someone answered the call. "Fireweed Restaurant, can you hold, please?"

"Of course."

As soon as the hold music began to play in my ear, I replied to Rosie. "They're not gonna gossip. They're going to deliver pizza, and it's really good. It will be here faster than it takes your frozen pizza to bake." I paused, listening to the music. "They need to change this," I muttered.

Rosie snorted before she turned and eyed the frozen pizza box she had pulled out of her freezer. "This says twenty-five minutes."

Before I could respond, the guy who had answered came back on the line. "Hi there, what can I get for you?"

"Hey, Dale, it's Wyatt. I don't normally pull rank, but I just told my friend that our pizza delivery time would beat the frozen pizza that is apparently supposed to take twenty-five minutes to cook. What are my odds of being right?"

Dale let out a dry chuckle. "Pretty good. We're busy, but our early rush is over. How far out are you?"

"Ten minutes, give or take a few."

"We can probably get it to you in fifteen or twenty.

Unless your order is something complicated," he replied.

Glancing at Rosie, I mouthed, "What kind of pizza do you want?"

"Pepperoni and mushroom."

A woman after my own heart, I thought. I almost repeated it aloud before catching myself. "Pepperoni and mushroom. That's simple, I think," I said to Dale.

"We keep those prepped, so you're good."

"Tell the driver to drive fast and take chances," I teased.

Dale's laughter filtered through the line before he said, "Nope, but it'll make it in time."

"No matter what, I'm gonna give them a killer tip."

When I hung up the phone, Rosie rolled her eyes. She put the frozen pizza back in the freezer. "I hope your odds are good. We should bet," she added.

"Oh, sweetheart, I'll bet."

Her eyes narrowed. "You will?"

"Absolutely. If I win, I get a night with you. Whenever I want. On my terms."

Before she opened her mouth to respond, I added, "As long as you're in the mood and want whatever I want and accept my terms at the time."

She pressed her lips together to keep from laughing. "Are you making sure this bet meets the standards of consent?"

"Sure am. I'm a modern man." My tone was light, but I was serious.

In a flash, the teasing mood shifted to sober as Rosie held my gaze. I watched as emotions danced in the depths of her eyes. "I don't like admitting this, but Wyatt Cannon, you just do it for me. I'm not worried about that. Ever."

Her words felt as if they slammed into my chest

and gripped my heart as I stared back at her. I knew what it cost her to be open and vulnerable to me or anyone. Maybe I didn't understand all of Rosie's heart, but I knew what I felt. Perhaps someday she would trust me enough to help me understand her more thoroughly.

Emotion tightened in my throat, and I actually had to clear my throat to speak. "I'm honored with your trust. I promise I'll protect it."

Chapter Fourteen

ROSIE

Hours later, I lay in the darkness. Wyatt's words played on repeat in my thoughts, complete with his gruff, somber tone. *I promise I'll protect it.*

He had already told me he loved me, and my heart didn't know how to believe it. I was still shocked at the depth of my own feelings. I loved Wyatt. It seemed too fast as if I'd lost my balance running downhill. I'd known him as long as I could remember. He had always been in the periphery of my life as a person who was safe and one of my closest friends.

The memories from that fated week before I went to nursing school had been burned into my body and mind. I hadn't been able to forget him. Everything with him during that week had just been *soooo* good.

At the time, I chalked it up to it being my first really good connection with someone on a physical level. I'd been focused on leaving for nursing school immediately after that, and those distractions had crowded my emotions around Wyatt out of the way. I'd also been worried about my dad and my brother. My dad was obviously a perfectly capable adult, but when you're the oldest child of two, and your only parent works a lot because they have to, it's not unusual to slip into a caretaking role. I had worried deeply about my brother with me moving away from town.

As my thoughts started to detour onto that track, I slammed on the brakes and yanked the wheel back onto Wyatt. It said something that I'd preferred to contemplate telling Wyatt I loved him, then let myself dwell on my worries for my brother.

I shifted in bed. During that week years back, Wyatt and I had slept together almost every night. The sleeping part, that is, along with the super-hot sexy times. He'd slept flat on his back or curled up around me.

At this moment, he slept on his side with his palm resting on my belly. Even in sleep, his touch was comforting. He had strong, capable hands.

I flushed as I lay there in the darkness. All it took was a subtle shift of his palm, and nothing more than the minuscule friction created by his calloused touch was a turn-on. Everything about Wyatt was a turn-on for me.

My mind circled back to when the pizza arrived just barely past fifteen minutes after Wyatt ordered it. He'd teased that tonight could count for him winning the bet. I straightened one of my legs where my knee had been bent. I didn't mean to, but it woke him. I could feel the subtle buzz of energy slide through him as his hand moved in a slow caress across my belly before settling in the center again.

"What are you worrying about, sweetheart?" His voice was low in the quiet darkness.

My body hummed. I might as well have been a

little cat purring in the darkness at nothing more than a brush of someone's fingertips under my chin.

"How do you know I'm worrying?" I hedged as my lips curled into a smile.

"I can practically hear you thinking."

I bit my lip, feeling bashful and grateful for the cover provided by the mostly dark bedroom. Maybe it was because it was the middle of the night. Maybe it was because my heart was determined to shout out my doubts for once, but the truth slipped out.

"I love you."

Wyatt went completely still. It wasn't as if he'd been moving much, but the silence suddenly became loaded, vibrating with emotions and our thoughts banging around inside our own heads and hearts.

He cleared his throat. "Well, you know I love you."

My heart pounded so hard I could hardly breathe. I managed a small sip of air before whispering, "That's what you said."

"Twice," he said, his voice low and clear. "For what it's worth, I think once is enough, but just in case you didn't hear me say it before."

I turned over, curling toward him to see his face better. "I heard you that night."

"So what's got you worrying about this in the middle of the night now?"

His eyes held mine, his gaze direct and holding a tenderness that nearly cracked my heart wide open.

I swallowed and cleared my throat. "Since we're being honest, it's what you said earlier about trust. I wanted to tell you I loved you then, but I didn't."

"You don't have to tell me anything. I hope you know that."

"I know. I want to." I let out something between a laugh and a sigh. "I think we did this all backward."

"What do you mean?" he asked.

"Well, we're already married."

His chuckle was low and sent warmth spinning around my heart. "We are. I knew that night I loved you. Since we're being honest, I'll admit I didn't plan that night. And before it all started, I didn't know I loved you in the sense of really consciously knowing. I just knew I'd never forgotten you after our week together. But life happened and all that. Once we were together again, I knew."

"So what do we do now?"

"I say we do what we said we were going to do. We see how this goes. I think we're both cynical enough to know that just because people are in love and married doesn't always mean things work out."

His honesty was spot-on, but it stung a little. Because the part of my heart that had finally shouted out above the cacophony of doubts and cynicism was feeling very hopeful. *Of course it would all work out. Right?*

My mind spun back in time to the nights I'd woken to hear my father's quiet sobs in the days after my mother died. Even when love bound people together, you couldn't trust that it would work out.

I was an action-oriented person. Now that I'd gone and thrown my feelings out there, I wanted to *do* something about them. The little girl who had lost her mom, that part of me wanted promises and certainty and guarantees. I wanted love, faith, commitment, and happily ever after.

"You're thinking again, Rosie," Wyatt whispered as he dipped his head and brushed a kiss on my lips.

I let out a sheepish sigh. I *was* thinking, and that tended to get in the way.

When I shifted a little, I became aware of two

details. The arousal slick between my thighs and the velvety hard length of him where my knee brushed against it. Even when I wasn't focused on it, being naked with Wyatt set the banked embers of desire flickering inside.

"You can ignore that," he said.

I placed my hand on his heart, savoring its strong and rapid beat against my palm. "What if I don't want to?"

"In that case, sweetheart, you just tell me what you want."

The promise contained in his words was irresistible. My need trampled over anything else. If I was with anyone other than Wyatt, maybe this would've been different. But the desire between us was its own force and heightened by my love for him.

I shimmied a little closer and leaned up to press hot, open kisses on the underside of his jaw. His hand slid into my hair, and seconds later, he claimed my mouth. I felt like I tumbled into a sweet, fiery-hot fever dream. Our kisses were lazy and deep. I felt almost intoxicated, everything a slow blur. *That* was the effect Wyatt had on me.

One kiss slipped into the next. Wyatt's hands mapped my body, his touch, strong and sure. I molded myself to him, rolling over on top of him and savoring the slide of his palm down my back and the way he squeezed my bottom. He nipped at my neck and shivers raced down my side.

I had lost all sense of time when we finally broke apart, both of us breathing raggedly. I stared into his eyes in the hazy darkness. He whispered something. I couldn't even decipher the words, but I knew they were good.

He smoothed my hair away from my face, and I

moved to rise. I straddled him, his hard length nestled against my slippery, wet core. He shifted back slightly, propping himself against the pillows.

"Fuck," he muttered.

"What is it?" I whispered.

"I need a condom."

He moved to lift me off him, but I cut in, "I have an IUD."

He stared at me, lifting a hand to palm my cheek. "Are you sure?"

"Oh, I'm very sure I have an IUD." I bit my lip to keep from laughing.

A glint of mirth entered his gaze as he studied me. "No, I meant, are you sure you don't want me to use a condom? That's a reasonable question," he pointed out.

I felt a little bashful as I looked back at him. "I am sure. I trust you, I mean, if..."

"To make it completely clear, yes, I trust you," he added.

My pulse raced along, a wild fluttering in my chest. It wasn't just my need for him that had my heart thumping so madly. It was this intimacy, this vulnerability, the way my emotional walls fell away when I was with him.

I drew in a shaky breath. His other palm slid down my back, coming to rest between my shoulder blades, just behind my heart as he levered me forward. My forehead fell to his when our lips met in a slow, sensual tangle of tongues. My hips reflectively rocked, sliding back and forth over the underside of his cock. With his length nestled between my folds, I rode my clit over him. The friction created by the subtle motion pushed me straight to the edge of my control with pleasure tightening inside me almost unbearably.

We broke apart, our lips brushing as he spoke, "Let me be inside you."

I nodded incrementally and rose slightly. He reached between us, positioning his thick crown at my entrance. I could barely breathe because of the anticipation humming through me. His hips moved, rolling up as I slid down and sheathed him in the very heart of me.

I seated myself fully, and he nudged upward a little deeper. With his eyes on mine and his hands gripping my hips, we rocked together. The intense friction created from the slow motion, right where we were joined, sent pleasure shooting through me in piercing streaks. He reached between us, his thumb teasing over my swollen clit with just enough pressure to shatter through me.

I cried out, shuddering and trembling all over. I felt liquid melting inside when he kissed me, catching the last of my cries.

He moved, somehow spinning us over and shifting down on the bed. It was quick and a little messy, but he never once lost his hold on me. I savored his weight. He stretched my arms up over my head, gripping them with one hand. He murmured, "And now I'm going to fuck you just a little harder, sweetheart."

"Okay," I whispered.

He did just that with deep pumps inside me. It felt as if my orgasm just went on and on and on. I felt him tightening, his body a shivering stretch above me, with one last slow pump of his hips before I felt the heat of his release filling me as he cried my name in a guttural shout.

He collapsed against me for several thundering beats of my heart before he rolled to the side, holding me close against him when he slipped out of me. We lay there, our breathing slowing together. My palm had landed just over his heart, and I could feel his heartbeat gradually slow along with my own.

"I love you, Rosie," he rasped. He pressed a kiss to my forehead and one on each corner of my mouth.

I dragged my eyes open. "I love you, Wyatt."

I didn't recall falling asleep, but the last thing I remembered was a sense of sheer relief. That was followed by a feeling of comfort and safety that I couldn't ever remember feeling, except maybe before my mom died.

Chapter Fifteen

ROSIE

We were in the kitchen having coffee the following morning when there was a knock on my door. Alarm shot through me, and I glanced over at Wyatt. He sat at my kitchen table, fully dressed, but his hair was damp from a shower. It would be obvious to anyone that he had spent the night here.

He caught my eyes and shrugged. It would be my father or my brother. "Whatever," I said with a sharp sigh. I turned from where I'd stood at the kitchen counter, filling my coffee mug.

Walking over, I swung the door open, and my brother stood there. "Hey." Brent looked worried, shifting from one foot to the other. His hands were stuffed in the pockets of his jeans.

A gust of wind blew through the door, and I gestured for him to come in. "What's up?" I asked.

He let out a quick sigh before his eyes took in Wyatt and looped back to me. He didn't say anything. Wyatt dipped his chin in acknowledgment. "Morning, Brent."

My brother was tactful enough not to ask why

Wyatt was here. He glanced back toward me. "Dad needs a ride to an appointment today. I forgot, and I have to get to work."

I didn't know what the hell was going on, but I knew my brother was hiding something, and it bothered me. A lot. But now wasn't the time to get into that. "Okay, what time is his appointment?"

"Noon," Brent replied.

I reached for my phone on the counter and pulled up my work schedule. "I'll be at work, but I can have somebody cover for the hour." I was trying really hard not to get snippy with my brother. It would've been great if he had told me sooner, but I wasn't going to mention that now.

"Thanks. Good to see you, Wyatt," he said. With a quick wave, my brother was gone.

Wyatt held my gaze as I returned to the kitchen. "You okay?" he asked a moment later as I sat across from him.

I took a sip of coffee and shrugged. "I don't know. Something is going on with my brother, and it's driving me crazy."

"Kenan says he's doing great at work."

"I'm sure he is. I know I worry too much," I replied with a sigh. "I was eight when he was born, and my mom died."

"Your mom died when you were eight?"

I nodded. "She died from complications after Brent was born."

Wyatt's eyes widened slightly, with sadness and understanding flickering in his gaze. He had lost his father during his childhood. McKenna was one of the few friends when we were little who seemed to understand the kind of psychic blow it was to lose a parent.

"That must've been really hard," Wyatt offered carefully.

A familiar tightness clutched around my heart. I took a slow breath and swallowed through the thick feeling in my throat. "It was. I think you probably understand maybe more than most."

"I know it was really hard when our dad died."

"I'm sure it was. My dad did his best after my mom died, but he worked a lot. I helped out as much as I could with my brother. Brent left for college, and then he dropped out. Since he came home, he hasn't talked to me about it. I think he would like me not to worry about him so much."

Wyatt studied me, his gaze considering. "I don't think that has any..." He paused. "Let me clarify. I know what it's like to have older siblings. I have plenty of them, so I get it. Rhys was kind of a father to all of us. We dealt with some bullshit growing up."

"I know it wasn't easy."

"Although Jake was the oldest, he was a mess. Rhys was the one who was there for us. When I was a teenager, the last thing I wanted was advice from any of my older siblings. It's kind of normal when you're in high school, even earlier than that maybe. But still, I look up to every older sibling I have. It's just you and your brother. Even if it feels like Brent wants to shrug you off, he looks up to you. I don't doubt it for a minute. At the same time, he's probably going to be annoyed with anything you worry about. Give him a few more years, maybe sooner or maybe a little later, and he'll get past it. None of that has anything to do with you. He didn't have a mom. That's normal for that situation too. It's not easy."

I blinked away the tears stinging my eyes. I experienced a mixture of sadness and deep appreciation that

Wyatt grasped something that so many people didn't. When you lost a parent, it changed the entire dynamic in your family.

"I'm definitely not the oldest child in my family, but I have two younger siblings. I sort of understand the worry you deal with," he commented.

"So you're older than Griffin?" I couldn't help but ask.

Wyatt's lips curled in a small smile as he shrugged. "About fifteen minutes older. Being a twin is kind of weird. I suppose you're protective of each other no matter what. Griffin and I are protective of McKenna, so I can imagine just how protective you feel about your brother."

I pressed my lips together, twisting them to the side as I let out a little sigh. "I worry all the time. I worry that he parties too much. I worry that he's going to do something stupid. I worry that he drives too fast. I worry about all of it. It's breaking my dad's heart that Brent didn't want to help with the hardware store. My dad's slowing down a lot. He has people to help at the store, but still. When I went to get my nursing degree, my dad was going strong. I didn't think about what to do when he got older."

"You know, one way or another, it'll work out. Maybe your brother wants to handle the hardware store, or maybe he doesn't. You're doing enough. I certainly don't think you need to feel like it's on you to take over the hardware store."

I blinked back my tears. "I'm *really* relieved Brent picked up that job with Kenan. It seems like a good fit for him."

Wyatt chuckled. "It does. For someone who likes to stay busy and can roll with doing something different practically every day, it's nearly perfect."

Wyatt's cell phone vibrated, and he glanced at it where it sat on the counter. "Speaking of work, I'm gonna have to roll out in a few minutes."

My heart tightened a little in my chest. I wanted to ignore the feeling, but I'd already gone and told Wyatt I'd loved him. I couldn't believe it. I was going to miss him. It was just a day. He was going to work, I was going to work, and I was going to miss him.

"You okay?" he prompted.

I met his eyes and managed a smile. "I am."

I felt too sheepish and vulnerable to share how I felt just now. I suppose my emotions were heightened because we had just talked about my mom and all my worries about my brother. I carried those worries mostly alone. I knew my dad understood, but I tried not to burden him. Not only did he worry about my brother, but he worried about me worrying about my brother. He had enough going on, in addition to his health issues, without me piling on more.

A few minutes later, we left my house together. He stopped me between our cars and looked down at me, the intensity in his gaze burning into me. "Tell me when you want this to be something more than just between us."

"My brother already knows," I pointed out. I knew my brother wouldn't gossip. That was definitely not his style.

"I know, but I mean more than that."

My belly shimmied. Wyatt lifted a hand, smoothing it over the furrow forming in my brow. "You're worrying," he said softly before pressing a kiss there.

I bit my lip as I smiled up at him. "I do that."

"Think about it," he whispered before giving me a quick, fierce kiss on the lips.

Chapter Sixteen

WYATT

A few days later, after I had stolen one more night with Rosie, she looked up at me from where we stood between our vehicles again at her house. "You told me to tell you when I wanted this to be something more."

"I did," I said, my thumb twisting a lock of her auburn hair around my forefinger.

She took a quick breath as she shifted on her feet. "We don't have to keep it a secret."

"Are we telling people we actually got married in Vegas?"

She bit her lip. "I'm not sure about that part yet. Everybody will think we're crazy."

"Well, it *was* a little crazy," I pointed out.

She chewed on the inside of her cheek as she studied me. "It was a little crazy, but…"

"Let's just take it a step at a time."

A smile unfurled slowly across her face. "Yes, please. We can just be open that we're dating, and it's maybe sort of serious."

My heart thumped hard in my chest. I wanted more, *so* much more, but I checked that urge. "Okay, so how should we break the news? So far, your brother and Griffin know."

"And my dad," she said. "He saw your truck the other night when you were here. He won't say anything, and my brother hasn't said anything, and I can't believe Griffin hasn't said anything." She paused, rolling her eyes. "Oh, and the doctor you told when you got your stitches."

I grinned. "Doesn't seem like she's gossiped about us."

Rosie shook her head as she reached up to twirl a lock of her auburn hair around her fingers. She didn't show her nervousness much, but when it was evident, my heart twisted a little in my chest. She was so strong, so guarded, so protective of herself and of her heart.

"It's okay," I said softly.

"What's okay?" She blinked.

"Think of it this way." I stepped closer, reaching for her other hand. I held it in mine, brushing my thumb along the back of her palm before turning it over and dusting a kiss on the inside of her wrist. "When you found out Tessa and Adam were seeing each other, did you judge them? And what about McKenna and Jack? Or Blake and Fiona?"

"Don't forget Rhys and Haven," she interjected with a smile teasing the corners of her mouth.

"Of course not. And Kenan and Quinn?"

"I know, I know." She finally released the curl she'd been spinning around her fingers and let out a tiny huff as I coaxed her a little closer and reached for her other hand.

"What are you worried about?" I asked.

Her eyes glistened with a hint of tears, and my heart nearly cracked open. "That it will all blow up, or that it won't, and something bad will happen later."

"You mean something like what happened to your mom?"

She blinked before clearing her throat and nodding.

"Okay, okay. I understand." My voice was thick and husky. It wasn't that I denied the pain I'd experienced in losing my father, but I hadn't been alone in the echoing grief. She had her father, but the gap between her and her younger brother was large enough that she must've felt alone in her loss.

My family was a muddy mess of other shit that went down after my father passed. But still, I often kept my grief tucked away. Whenever I let myself feel it, and whenever it came up, like now, it was a piercing pain. It wasn't as awful and as encompassing as it had felt when I'd been a little boy, yet the loss was always there.

"I want to lie and tell you it will all be okay, but I can't do that. I know that there are no guarantees in life. I love you, and I want a chance with you. I think we might already be past the point of keeping it from hurting."

She cleared her throat again and took a slow breath before squeezing my hands. "I know that. And, well, we're married." Her lips curled into a wobbly smile.

A laugh rustled in my throat. "True. We have to file paperwork for a divorce and everything if we want to break up officially."

She rolled her eyes. "Can we at least give it a little time before we tell everyone we actually got married in Vegas? Except for Griffin, who I guess knows everything."

"Not everything," I replied. He did know most of

my story with Rosie, but he had no idea how much she meant to me. I suspected he couldn't understand that until he met someone who meant as much to him. "How do you want to handle this? How do we go public?" I asked.

She tipped her head to the side. "Well, there's locals' night coming up. We could meet there, and I could hold your hand."

"Just hold my hand? I'll kiss you if you let me," I teased. Her cheeks went pink. "Like this." I drew her closer to demonstrate and ended up making myself breathless by the time I lifted my head.

Chapter Seventeen

ROSIE

Me: *I told Tessa.*

Wyatt: *I figured. She told Adam, and he told me he'd suspected it.*

Me: *Tessa said the same thing! Are we that obvious?*

Wyatt: *Sweetheart, I've had it bad for you for years. The only reason it wasn't obvious before I moved home was that I wasn't here for anyone to notice.*

My cheeks burned, and I had to bite my lip to keep from smiling too hard.

Before I could respond, another text came in.

Wyatt: *How about you meet me at my office tonight?*

At the mere thought of the table in his office, my cheeks burned even hotter.

Me: *Okay.*

Wyatt: *Okay? Do you remember the last time you were in my office?*

Me: *How could I forget?*

Wyatt: *That's more like it. I'll be waiting.*

Thank goodness I had a job that kept my mind occupied. Otherwise, I would've spent the day dwelling on how to handle everyone knowing about Wyatt and me. Even then, they wouldn't know the whole truth.

As it was, the hospital was beyond hectic. That was par for the course in an emergency room, even in a small town in Alaska. By the time the end of my shift rolled around, I was running on fumes. I was relieved that it was locals' night. Not that I wanted to stay too late, but I could use the food and drinks just being handed to me so I didn't have to think. Wyatt's presence always soothed me after a long day. Although I had admitted to myself and to him just how much he meant to me, I shied away from pondering what it meant that he was the person I turned to when I needed comfort, the port in my personal storm.

I stepped into the bathroom in the small locker area for nurses. I splashed water on my face and whipped a brush through my hair before pulling it back up into a ponytail. My hair was beyond recovery for trying to leave it down. I changed out of my scrubs into a pair of cotton pants. They could pass for attractive, but they were mostly comfortable. They had a wide waistband and swung around my ankles. Atop that, I wore a comfortable long-sleeved cotton shirt. It was attractive enough, but all I wanted was comfort after a day like this one. On the list of reasons Wyatt mattered so much to me, I knew I didn't have to worry about going out of my way to look good for him. I could just be comfortable, and it wouldn't matter.

A short drive later, I parked behind the headquarters for Fireweed Industries. I smiled as I glanced toward Wyatt's truck when I climbed out. I told myself I didn't purposely park beside him. My teenage heart whispered, *Yes, you did,* in a singsong voice in my thoughts.

Moments later, I slipped into the back hallway at the brewery, wondering if I might see anyone as I hurried down the hall toward Wyatt's office. Just before I reached his doorway, Blake walked out of his office, which was directly across the hallway. Blake greeted me just as the door to Wyatt's office swung open.

Heat flashed into my cheeks. Blake cracked a quick grin as he glanced back and forth between us. "Oh, I see you two have finally come to your senses."

"Wh-wh-a-a-t?" I sputtered.

Blake arched a brow. "You two have been crushing on each other hard. I'm personally relieved to see you sneaking down here to visit Wyatt."

"Oh my God," I muttered under my breath.

Blake glanced toward Wyatt. "Adam told me."

"Of course he did," Wyatt said dryly.

Blake winked.

"I forgot how fast rumors travel through your family," I muttered.

"It's not a rumor," Blake pointed out with an insouciant shrug.

Wyatt let out a low chuckle, and heat prickled up my spine. Feeling put on the spot by Blake was no match for my body's reaction to Wyatt's mere presence.

"Adam said he heard it from Tessa because you told Tessa, so don't blame me," Blake added.

I narrowed my eyes at him. "Fine," I ground out. "Maybe that's what happened."

"Maybe?" Blake's return smile was warm and understanding. He loved to tease, but he was never unkind about it.

I let out a little sigh. Blake reached out and squeezed me lightly on the shoulder. "I get it. Going public with things is hard. Trust me, though, Wyatt's the one who's dating above his pay grade."

Wyatt barked out a laugh, entirely unbothered by his brother's teasing. "Maybe I am, and that is perfectly fine with me. I know how lucky I am."

Blake stepped farther into the hallway and shut his office door behind him. "Well, I'm sure I'll see you in the restaurant soon." With that, he winked at both of us and strolled down the hall, whistling along the way.

Once he disappeared through the swinging doors into the front area of the building, I glanced at Wyatt. "I think his whistle was mocking us."

"It definitely was." Wyatt reached for my hand, and inside of a hot second, he reeled me close and spun us into his office together, kicking the door shut behind him.

"Oh!" I exclaimed a little breathlessly.

He took a step closer, nudging me backward as he did. I felt my shoulder blades press against the door. He bent low, dipping his head and pressing open kisses on the side of my neck. I was instantly hot all over. Wyatt turned me into a needy woman. It didn't take much.

When he nipped lightly on my skin, I literally shivered in the cage of his arms. He took another step closer, and I felt his heat press against the front of me. His hard length nestled at the apex of my thighs, just above where I wanted it. Moisture gushed into my panties.

He lifted his head. "You make me crazy, Rosie," he rasped.

"You make me needy," I whispered, shifting on my feet.

He rocked his hips, and I actually let out a little moan.

"How was your day?" he asked, his tone conversational.

His knuckles trailed along the side of my neck before the pad of his thumb slid across my collarbone. It felt like the lick of a flame on the surface of my skin, the subtle touch sending heat spiraling through me.

I took a shaky breath. "It was busy. How was yours?" I could hardly focus. Meanwhile, he seemed to be genuinely interested in how I was doing and how my day went. When all I wanted was... I couldn't even think.

"Could you just fuck me, please?"

Wyatt's eyes widened slightly before his lips curled in a slow, teasing grin.

"Of course, I can. You literally mean right now?"

Since I couldn't speak again, I nodded. Without hesitation, he lifted me into his arms. A moment later, he had me bent over the table again.

Chapter Eighteen

WYATT

A little while later

Rosie's cheeks were flushed when she stood in front of my office door. "Do I look okay?" she asked.

I took the moment to soak her in. The tendrils of hair falling around her cheeks. The way her freckles stood out a little more when her cheeks were flushed. Her kiss-swollen lips. She was dressed unremarkably in soft cotton pants and a long-sleeved T-shirt. Rosie was so *it* for me that I didn't ever notice what she was wearing beyond occasionally when I was simply taking in all of her.

"Fuck, I love you," I muttered. My heart swelled in my chest as I stepped closer and gave her a fierce kiss.

When I lifted my head, she blinked. "I love you too. What was that for?"

I shrugged. Even though I'd been open with her about my feelings, their intensity still startled me. "I was looking at you, and that's all I wanted to say."

"You didn't answer my first question yet," she teased.

I tucked a lock of hair behind her ear. "You look beautiful."

"I think I'm going to have to be more specific." She pressed her lips together and let out a little sigh. "Do I look like you just fucked me in your office?"

I chuckled. "I think I'm biased because I *know* I just fucked you in my office, and it was incredible."

She rolled her eyes. "You're no help." She reached for the doorknob. "Okay, let's do this."

"Tell me how we're handling this," I said as we walked down the hallway. I held her hand in mine because I couldn't bear not to touch her.

"I think everybody already knows, so we're just gonna pretend everybody already knows." She stopped abruptly, the soles of her shoes squeaking on the floor as she turned to face me. "Except for the marriage part."

"The marriage part?" A voice reached us from behind.

Rosie's breath sucked in sharply, and she spun around. Rhys was approaching. He must've come in through the back entrance. I felt flat-footed and caught off guard.

"You got married in Vegas," Rhys said matter-of-factly as he stopped beside us.

"What?!" Rosie yelped.

Rhys's gaze was understanding as he studied her. "It's okay. I won't say anything. Well, I told Haven I thought you were already married, but that's it."

I elected to stay silent. When Rosie looked wildly at me, two bright red spots high on her cheeks, Rhys took pity on us. "Wyatt's not saying anything because he's afraid you're gonna get mad at whatever he says.

The only reason I suspected the marriage part is because in Vegas, I saw you two coming out of one of the wedding chapels there. Haven had lost her purse along the way that night, so I went to find it."

"You've known this whole time?" Rosie's mouth dropped open.

Rhys shrugged. "I can keep a secret. I wasn't *sure*, well, except for the fact you almost fell over on the sidewalk and you were both wearing rings. You never even saw me, and I was maybe twenty feet away."

I looked at Rhys, giving him a nod. "Damn. You definitely know how to hold your cards close to your chest."

Rosie leaned her head back and bounced her heel on the floor as she let out a groan of frustration. When she leveled her eyes with mine again, she looked resigned.

"Rhys won't say anything," I assured her.

"I haven't said anything to anybody yet except Haven," he pointed out.

Rosie looked from Rhys to me, to the floor, to the ceiling, and then back at me. "You know what? Fuck it."

"Uh, fuck what?" I asked.

"We'll just tell everyone. We got drunk, and we had a night in Vegas. It was crazy and now we're seeing how things go."

"Congratulations," Rhys said with an amused chuckle as he pulled me into a backslapping hug before hugging Rosie as well.

When he stepped back, Rosie looked up at him. "Are we crazy?"

"No crazier than anybody else I know," Rhys said easily. "I mean that," he added when she eyed him doubtfully. "Let me help."

"Help how?" I asked.

"Well, we all know you're together now, but when we go out, I'll make a toast to celebrate your marriage."

Rosie considered this quietly before nodding decisively. "Let's. I hate secrets. They stress me out."

Chapter Nineteen

WYATT

"You're married?" McKenna yelped, her mouth dropping open.

Rosie's cheeks were pink, and she shrugged as she smiled sheepishly. "Um, it was a Vegas thing."

McKenna's hands flew to her mouth. She stared at us before they fell. "I knew something was going on with you two, but even I didn't guess *that*."

She spun to look at Rhys, who had just toasted us. He winked over at Rosie and me before glancing back toward McKenna. "You knew?" My little sister's tone was accusatory.

"I didn't know for sure," Rhys clarified. "I suspected. And it turns out I was right. I'm thrilled for them, aren't you?"

McKenna's gaze softened. "Of course."

Family and friends made a few more toasts as conversation carried on around us. My mom came over to hug us and held both of Rosie's hands in hers. "I am thrilled for you and Wyatt."

"You are?" Rosie sounded surprised.

My mother nodded. "Most definitely. Honestly, I

never mentally paired you two together, but now that I know you're…" She paused before she beamed. "Married. It just feels right." Her eyes slid to me. "Wyatt is strong-willed, and he needs someone like you."

"What's your point, Mom?" I teased as I curled an arm around her shoulders and gave her a squeeze.

"My point is precisely that," she replied tartly. "Rosie won't hesitate to stand up to you, and she'll take care of your heart."

I could feel the sting of tears in my eyes as I looked down at my mother. I knew I needed to come clean soon with the whole story.

Chapter Twenty

ROSIE

A few mornings later

When I walked outside, I noticed my brother leaving early. I told myself I wasn't trying to keep tabs on Brent. It's just that I always worried. For the life of me, I couldn't figure out why he would be leaving this early. It was a foggy morning with the mist hanging heavy in the air.

This was the day I usually went to the transfer station, which was the only reason I happened to be outside loading the trash in the back of my car.

Brent glanced over. It looked as if I caught him doing something when all he was doing was leaving early.

"I know things are wild when you're up at this hour," I quipped.

His expression was pinched.

"Is everything okay?" I asked.

"Oh yeah," he said quickly. He paused as he opened

his car door, resting an elbow on the rooftop. "How are you and Wyatt?"

I didn't want to assume he was trying to change the subject, but it sure felt like it. But then, this was my brother and he liked to tease. Regardless of his reasons, it was an effective distraction. I was relieved for the gray, barely light morning and the cool air. It might've masked the heat that flared in my cheeks.

"We're fine, thanks for asking."

Brent studied me for a moment, his gaze considering. "I think he's good for you."

"You do?"

"I do. You carry a lot. You don't have to do it alone."

I didn't even know what to make of that comment. He tapped his fingers on the roof of his car. "Nobody has to do it all alone. I gotta roll. Love you, sis."

A moment later, I watched the taillights of his car fade into the mist as he drove away. I stood beside the back of my car, feeling discombobulated. My little brother was grown up, and I didn't even know what to make of that. For crying out loud, he was giving me advice about romance.

I slowly turned to close the hatch on my car before walking back into my house. I'd worked late last night and recalled getting home and being relieved my brother's car was parked in the driveway. I didn't want to worry so much about him, but it was like a muscle memory in my brain. I just did it. Like when I went to brush my teeth, I always started on the same side of my mouth.

I'd missed Wyatt last night and pondered his comment when he'd kissed me good night the night before that. "Everyone knows we're married now. We could just, you know, behave like we're married."

"What does that mean?" I'd lobbed back at him.

Wasn't that the million-dollar question? What did *that* mean?

The thing was, I would've happily had Wyatt with me every night. But it still terrified me a little to believe in us. It almost would've been easier—okay, definitely easier—if I hadn't gone and fallen in love with him like a foolish girl.

A few minutes later, I walked the short distance from my small house to the main house to check on my dad.

"Hello?" I called, peering inside as I opened the door.

"Hey, Rosie girl," he returned, his voice sounding surprisingly chipper.

I closed the door behind me and walked into the kitchen, where he was seated at the table. "Brent left early," I said by way of greeting.

Something passed through my father's gaze, but it didn't look concerning, so I let it be. "He did. He's loving his job with Kenan at Fireweed Industries. That man's got him running all over the place. It keeps him busy, and busy is good."

"You think?" I teased as I sat down across from him. "If that's the case, I am kicking ass at life."

My dad's gaze was warm, and his smile crinkled the corners of his eyes. "You are kicking ass at life, Rosie." He lifted his coffee mug. "Also, congratulations on your marriage."

A startled laugh slipped out. "The news is out."

My dad's gaze sobered as he looked over at me. "Wyatt Cannon is a good man. I think he's good for you."

"You do?"

He took a swallow of coffee, appearing to ponder

something in his thoughts before he set his mug down. "Yes. Your mother dying was really hard on you for lots of obvious reasons. You've never said it out loud, but I'm pretty sure you decided you would never need anyone after we lost her."

The breath I drew in was sharp as I pressed a palm to my chest, almost as if I needed to contain the sudden throb of pain in my heart. "Dad..."

"Rosie, don't worry about me. Losing your mom was devastating for me. Because I loved her. But you slowly get used to loss, and I've had plenty of time." He paused and tipped his head to the side slightly. "As far as I can tell, you decided love wasn't worth the risk. I promise you, it is."

Sometimes it hurt when someone knew you as well as my father knew me. Right now, my heart felt raw, as if a scab I'd forgotten about had been ripped off. The old pain felt exposed and fresh.

I took a shaky breath. "I don't know what to say."

"I don't think any of that was conscious on your part, for what it's worth. I'm just glad you're giving Wyatt a chance. I heard the whole story of Vegas and all that." He waved a hand in the air. "Maybe it was impulsive. Sometimes impulsive choices are stupid, but sometimes they lead us in the right direction and give us a chance not to dwell too much. Knowing you the way I do, I'm pretty sure if you didn't impulsively give somebody a chance, you would never give them a chance. That's all I'm saying."

I blinked away my tears. "I love you, Dad," I said when I thought I could speak without bawling my eyes out.

"I love you, he said solemnly. For what it's worth, I appreciate you worrying about your brother and me and making sure everything's okay. Your brother's doing a pretty good job checking on me. We're gonna work out a schedule where I can be at the hardware store, and he can pick me up and drop me off. It's good you don't have to carry everything alone."

As I drove to work later that day, I pondered that both my brother and father had made the same obser-vation—that I didn't have to carry things alone.

Chapter Twenty-One

WYATT

The door in the hallway swung open with a few people filtering out of a conference room. I stepped back. I happened to be in the basement over at our headquarters. We used some of the rooms down here for storage for the brewery. I was checking out some of the old equipment that my grandmother used for the wines. She didn't get out much these days, but she'd stopped by to see how things were going and had given me a few pointers on the production for the meads.

I was in a storage room across from one of the conference rooms. For years, we allowed these rooms to be available for AA and NA meetings. As bad luck would have it, I looked up just as Rosie's younger brother walked out of a meeting. His eyes met mine instantly.

I prepared to pretend I didn't even see him, but he barreled through that. He crossed the hallway and entered the room where I was. I was trying to give the people leaving some privacy as they came out of what was supposed to be an anonymous meeting.

"Hey," I offered, striving to keep my tone nonchalant.

"Hey. No sense in sneaking around. I go to NA meetings, but I've been clean and sober for a year and a half. Kenan knows. I went to an actual rehab program for sixty days after I dropped out of college. I moved home after that. Seeing as you're married to Rosie, I'm not gonna ask you to keep it a secret, but she'll probably freak right the hell out if she finds out."

I must've looked as flat-footed as I felt because Brent grinned a little. "Too heavy for you."

"Oh, I can handle it," I finally said. "I'm sure you know our family history, so dealing with heavy stuff isn't new to me. I guess I just wasn't expecting it in an instant dose like that from you. Does Rosie know anything about this at all?"

Her brother sort of shook his head and shrugged at the same time. "No, but maybe. The other day, Kenan and I had to take a trip to Juneau early. I went to an early morning meeting so I didn't miss it for the day. That's the kind of thing that would make her worry and wonder what was up. To be clear, I'm not bitching about her. My mom died right after I was born, so Rosie's the closest thing I have to a mom."

His tone was serious. The love in his voice scraped over my heart because I knew what it might mean for Rosie to hear that from him.

"Rosie worries about me. All the time." He continued. "She thought I made a mistake when I dropped out of college. If she knew I'd dropped out to go to rehab, she would lose her fucking mind."

"I understand," I finally said. "I know she doesn't like secrets." I hadn't forgotten how much it had bothered her to try to keep the secret that we were married. She flat-out said she hated secrets. And holy hell, *this* wasn't a secret I wanted to keep. But it wasn't my secret, and I knew it was Brent's to keep or tell.

I eyed him for a few beats. "I don't want to keep this from her," I finally said.

"And I understand that." He leaned his head back, looking up at the ceiling. The hallway had fallen quiet since the rest of the people in the meeting had filtered out and gone upstairs. "I'd like to tell her myself. Can you give me a week or so?"

I could live with that. "I can handle that. For what it's worth, it's not like I want to tell on you. I just know that it would hurt Rosie if she knew that I knew—"

Her brother cut in. "It would break her heart. She would be really hurt, and I don't want to keep this from her forever. I'll tell her." He paused, bouncing his heel on the floor. "If, for some insane reason, it comes up some other way, I will make sure she knows that I asked you to give me time to tell her myself."

Brent turned to go, but I reached out, catching him lightly by the elbow.

"Yeah?" He spun back.

"I know it can't be easy for you. You sure as hell don't have to give me all the details, but for what it's worth, I'm impressed by and proud of anyone who goes into recovery. It's not easy. We lost our oldest brother to alcohol poisoning."

Rosie's brother blinked before he nodded. "I know. I will never pretend it's easy, but I appreciate that. I hope I've gotten through the worst of it. Just one day at a time now. To start, it was one minute at a time. I just gotta remember that I can never get too relaxed about it."

I pulled him into a quick hug because it seemed

like the thing to do. When we broke apart, he grinned at me. "Wow, I'm hug-worthy."

"Absolutely. You're family."

He chuckled, and I watched as he walked away. It wasn't my secret to tell, but I sure as hell hoped I didn't have to keep it for him for too long.

After Brent jogged up the stairs, my thoughts circled his situation. I knew well what it meant for someone to face addiction. Our oldest brother had for years. To this day, I wrestled with a jumble of emotions about him. They were constantly bouncing into each other. Jake had borne the worst of what our grandfather had doled out. Yet he turned that anger outward toward our sister. As a result, I'd hated part of him for much of my life while also experiencing a messy mix of loving him and wishing things had been different.

Jake had been the person who taught me that nobody was all one thing or another. Good people make bad choices sometimes and hurt others, and the reverse could also be true. My mind detoured back to a well-worn path. I'd been in high school, and he'd been home for a visit. McKenna was in middle school at the time. She'd argued with him about something small, and he'd slapped her so hard, that the force of it whipped her head to the side and left a bright red imprint on her cheek for over an hour.

The next day, I'd approached him. "You're a fucking asshole."

He'd spun around and glanced over his shoulder. Because I was past the age he'd been now, I knew how young he was then even though he'd seemed all grown up to me. He'd been just old enough to call himself a man but wounded and damaged. I could picture him so clearly. He'd never gotten past that age where the contours of his face became sharper. He'd been lanky and thin.

"Yeah, I know I'm an asshole. Tell me something I don't know," he'd sneered.

"Don't ever fucking hit her again," I'd said. I was the tallest in our family, taller than him by then even though I was just a freshman in high school.

He'd stared back at me. "What the fuck are you talking about?"

"You bullying McKenna. Just fuck off. You're just like our grandfather." I knew now what I hadn't known then. Our grandfather had raped Jake. None of us would ever know if it was more than once because Jake was dead. We didn't find out until after he died. Our cousin had walked into the wrong room at the wrong time once and later shared it with the rest of us after years of experiencing panic attacks.

Now, when I pictured Jake's face, the guilt was even worse than it had been before. Because I understood how much pain he was in and what it meant for me to say he was just like our grandfather.

"Fuck you all," he'd muttered before turning and walking away.

That was the extent of my confrontation with him. He never bullied McKenna again because he died the next day.

I heard footsteps approaching and took a slow breath, willing the adrenaline coursing through my body to ease up.

"There you are." Rhys's voice reached me from the doorway.

Glancing over my shoulder, I tried to keep my tone casual. "Looking for me?"

He studied me for a moment before asking, "You okay?"

Maybe it was my conversation with Rosie's brother, but I couldn't keep the truth from bubbling up. "I confronted Jake the day before he drank himself to death. It was about the way he treated McKenna."

Rhys's hand had been resting on the inside of the doorframe, and it fell away as he stared at me. "Oh," he said

"I'm sorry."

"It's not your fault Jake drank himself to death. He partied hard in college." Rhys took another step into the room. "Is this why you've kept your distance all this time?"

"What do you mean?"

"Just that. I understand you had reasons that have nothing to do with that, but I always felt like I was missing something."

I took a quick breath, turning and resting my hips against the table cluttered with supplies. "I guess so." I shrugged one shoulder. "I always felt bad. I know how close you and Jake were."

"We were, but I knew he had a temper. I didn't know about the way he treated McKenna until that all came out. I'm glad you confronted him. If I'd known then, I would've too."

"It wasn't like I was planning to fight him. I just wanted him to know I knew and to back the fuck off. I didn't know he would die the next day. I also told him he was like our grandfather, and I hate that I said that."

Rhys took a quick breath, his tongue pressing into his cheek as he considered my words. "Look, it happened. You can't blame yourself for his drinking problem. We can't change the past. I hope to God you haven't blamed yourself all this time."

"I can intellectualize it, but it's always been there

in the back of my thoughts. It was only the next night that he died."

My brother's cheeks puffed out when he let out a big sigh. "Jake was responsible for his own choices. I think life was a fucking mess for him. We all understand better now why he drank so hard and partied so hard. He just wanted to forget, I think." Rhys took another step, placing his hands on my shoulders as I straightened and pushed away from the table. "It wasn't your fault. It's a miracle he didn't drink himself to death before that. There was more than one night when I had to help him back to his dorm and make sure he was okay. Blackout drunk was a fairly common state for him in those days."

I swallowed through the tight pain in my throat. "Maybe so, but I just wanted you to know."

"Are you gonna tell Mom?"

I pondered it for a moment before I shrugged. "I don't know. It felt more important to make sure you knew. I'm not sure how she would take it."

Rhys tipped his head to the side. "I don't know either. It was enough for her to accept how Jake treated McKenna. I don't think her knowing this is going to be any more hurtful than what she already knows. She's had to come to terms with the reality that she couldn't protect us from our grandfather when we were younger. She couldn't protect Jake and everything that happened set in motion a chain of events. The way Jake treated McKenna wasn't okay. At all. I think it's good that you confronted him. I honestly—and I really mean this—do not believe that's the reason he drank himself to death. He made partying a lifestyle, and it wasn't just alcohol. The amount of substances in his system that night was so significant they couldn't even say they knew which one killed him. He met the level for alcohol poisoning, but he had opiates and more thrown in the mix. He was running inside, trying to forget everything."

The tight place I'd held inside my chest for so many years loosened slightly. Maybe Rhys couldn't give me absolution, but it was a relief to talk to him and to hear him point out the obvious truth of Jake's life.

"Thank you," I said gruffly.

"For what?"

I cleared my throat. "For this. For letting me tell you and for not being angry."

He pulled me into a quick hug, squeezing me fiercely before he stepped back. "It's just the truth."

We walked upstairs together. After that, I left to talk to our mom because I was in the mind frame to handle it and buoyed a little by Rhys's assurances.

Chapter Twenty-Two

WYATT

It was always strange to walk into our childhood home. A mix of emotions rushed into me whenever I did. We had all grown up here, and the bond we formed as a messy cluster of siblings was strong. There were so many good memories here because we loved each other. When our dad was here, there were good memories with him. I'd been young when he passed, but even then, I could still remember a little, mostly a feeling of security. Following that were the dark days of our grandfather. The flip side of his cruelty was bonding us together even more tightly. Except for Jake.

"Hi," my mom said warmly when I walked into the kitchen.

I had texted that I was on the way over. I leaned over and dropped a kiss on her cheek before rounding the kitchen counter to slide my hips onto a stool across from her.

"Coffee?" she asked.

I glanced down to see a mug sitting immediately in

front of me. "I think you think I'm gonna say yes," I teased.

She grinned. "Possibly. So what brings you here today?"

"I can't just stop by to say hi?" I hedged.

My mother angled her head to the side. "You could, but I suspect there's more to it than that. Just a feeling, I suppose."

I took a swallow of coffee as I contemplated the best way to say what I needed to say. I didn't let myself dwell long. Maybe it was because I didn't want to think about it too much. The urge to just spill it pressed forcefully.

"I know you know about the way Jake treated McKenna," I began.

"Of course I do. We talked about it. Is there something else?" My mother's gaze shifted to trepidatious.

My heart ached a little. She had carried a lot. Our father's passing, our grandfather's actions, and carrying her own guilt about not knowing how to push back on that and protect us from him, especially Jake. And then, Jake dying. It was all just a big mess, and it felt like the vine of the poison from our grandfather was still tangled in our family. Its tendrils reached far.

I took a quick breath. "I confronted Jake about the way he treated McKenna the day before he died."

As my mother stared back at me, my thoughts shot back to that afternoon. I was just a kid, just old enough to stand up to Jake, to have a voice. But I'd still been just a kid. He'd been a senior in college, and I'd been a freshman in high school. My body was ahead of my brain back then. I was tall and could easily pass as a young adult. Yet inside I'd been a boy who wanted to keep his little sister safe.

My mother was quiet for several beats before she

let out a sharp sigh. "Ever since McKenna told me what happened, I wondered."

"If I confronted him?"

She nodded. "I didn't hear what you said to him, but I heard him tell you to fuck off, or something like that before he stormed out." She let out a weary sigh. "Before I say more, I want you to know I started seeing a therapist. I went to her after Jake died, and I started going again recently. I needed to understand better why I idolized Jake even though I knew he wasn't perfect. He had a terrible temper. And—" Another sigh, this one ragged. "I just... I feel like I failed all of you. Your father died, and I kind of fell apart. I was numb. Your grandmother was a big help, but I didn't realize what your grandfather did. I knew he had a temper, but I chalked it up to the yelling. Even then, I was in a cloud. To this day, I wonder what your father didn't tell me. His generation was different. Maybe you don't understand that, and I can't expect you to. It doesn't matter, even if you do. He would say things here and there about his father being hard to deal with, but—" She shrugged a little. "I don't know. I don't know what it meant. I think he went through more than I can understand and will ever be able to know. I would hope he would've told me if his father had done to him what he did to Jake, but I don't know. I know I never saw your father lose his temper with any of you."

She paused, and I could see the questions swirling in her eyes. I had been four when our father died. The memories I had were little bits and pieces, maybe a snapshot here and there of more feelings than concrete events. "I don't remember much, Mom. But I don't remember any bad feelings about him."

"Your grandfather was usually here when I wasn't."

"Yeah. You were working, Grandma was working, and he worked. It seemed like one of you was always here, but never more than one of you. There were a lot of us to take care of."

My mother's smile was sad and warm at the same time. "I know. I certainly hope you don't blame yourself. Jake was hurting badly. I knew he had a drinking problem, but I didn't know what to do about it."

My throat was tight as I nodded. "I guess I just wanted it out there."

My mother straightened on her stool, her shoulders rising and falling with a deep breath. I took another sip of my coffee, that old familiar tightness in my chest easing even more. I didn't expect absolution. I suppose I was realizing something I'd known all along. It wasn't my fault that Jake died, but I'd carried some guilt around the events for prodding at him. None of us had known the whole story back then, and maybe we still didn't. "I'm not sure why I told you," I finally said. "I guess I just wanted you to know. I talked to Rhys too."

"Did he tell you to come talk to me?" she asked.

I shook my head. "I think it was something I needed to do."

My mother slipped off her stool and rounded the counter to me, pulling me into a quick hug as I stood to meet her. When she stepped back, she squeezed my shoulders, looking deeply into my eyes. "You were always such a good boy. I'm grateful you were there to protect McKenna. I will always miss Jake, but I miss the best parts of him. I suppose we're all kind of broken and hurt in our own ways."

"We are. I miss him too. I don't miss his anger, but I miss him."

She returned to her seat, and we nursed our coffees

quietly for a few minutes. I was surprised when Griffin showed up.

My mother smiled. "Telepathy?" she teased lightly.

Griffin chuckled as he kissed her on the cheek before sitting down. Glancing back and forth between us, he rested his elbows on the counter.

My mother got up and walked across the kitchen to fetch a mug, calling over, "Coffee?"

He chuckled. "Well, I don't wanna feel left out."

A moment later, he had his coffee, and my mother was seated again. "So how much longer do I get your sweet face in town?"

"If you're gonna call me 'sweet,' I may have to leave sooner," Griffin quipped.

I grinned over at him. "She just called me a good boy. You can handle being called sweet."

Griffin kicked my calf and took a swallow of coffee. "I'm leaving in the fall."

My mother nodded. "Good."

"Good?" I prompted.

She smiled at us. "I knew he wasn't going to stay. He's not done firefighting. And it fits for him to go to Willow Brook. We need someone there. He can do the firefighting, and when he's ready, he can help with the brewery there."

"I can?" Griffin prompted

My mother laughed softly. "Well, yes. A lot is going on with the expansion, the restaurant, and eventually the brewery location that will be there. You can't fight fires forever, but you can do that for a couple of years, and then when you get over your death wish, you can be in charge of the brewery there. I know my boys, and you all have different personalities, but you are the most like Wyatt." She cast me a quick smile.

Griffin nodded thoughtfully, tracing his fingertip

around his mug on the counter. "Maybe. For now, I like fighting fires."

"And you'll get to run a whole crew there. That's a good deal," I pointed out.

"So what's up?" Griffin asked next.

My mother looked between us. "I'm sure you already know the whole story."

Griffin quickly read the look on my face. "Well, good. It's always nice to have the whole truth out there."

Chapter Twenty-Three

WYATT

A week later, I was reminded of Griffin's observation. Rosie's brother still hadn't told her. I fucking hated that I was waiting.

It wasn't my secret to tell, but I also didn't want to keep anything from her. Things with us were good. *Really* good. We'd spent every night together since we decided to stop sneaking around even though she was still wearing her wedding ring tucked under her shirt.

One night, I let my fingertips trail down the soft skin of her neck and along the slender chain of her necklace. I caught the ring in my fingers. It was cheap and thin. I wished I could remember actually picking it out. All I had were little snapshots of that night. I recalled her holding her hand up as we laughed together.

"Everyone knows we're married now," I pointed out.

She rolled her head to the side, smiling at me. "I know. I thought maybe we'd wait until we were sure."

"When will we know that? Because I know. I'm sure."

I literally felt the vulnerability that flickered in her eyes in my own heart. She took a quick breath. I rolled over to face her more fully, smoothing a loose lock of hair off her cheek to tuck behind her ear. "Tell me what you're worried about."

She let out a disbelieving laugh. "Um, I mean, everything?"

"Sweetheart, I don't think you worry about everything. I've seen you at the hospital. You are super-efficient, unruffled, and totally in control of one crisis after another."

Her lips curled in a soft smile. She lifted her hand to trace over the fairly fresh scar from the fish hook in my shoulder.

"You've seen me at the hospital once."

"I've seen you more than that," I pointed out. "I haven't personally been injured that often, but I've stopped by here and there. You know what I mean." My voice was low.

Her chest rose and fell with the slow breath she took. "My dad was devastated when my mom died. And honestly, that's something I worry about. What if the same thing happens to me? Or just anything? Lots of things can go wrong in life. I don't understand how it's so easy for you."

"What's so easy for me?"

She circled her hand in the air. "Being so confident about being in love. Thinking it'll be okay. What if it's not?"

"It's not that I don't worry, sweetheart. I do. Obviously, I'd be devastated if something happened to you. We're different, but we both have our reasons to understand life isn't always easy. It's just... I love you. I'm willing to do the hard part to have this with you."

"Do you want to—" Her words cut off.

"Have it all?" I finished, not sure that's what she meant to say, but it's what I felt.

She blinked. There was a sheen of tears in her eyes as she studied me. "I guess it's already gone too far."

"Because we're married?"

She rolled her eyes a little, letting out a tiny snort. "No, because I fell in love with you."

"Ah, so we're already in the danger zone?"

Her fingers walked their way down from my shoulder onto my chest where she began to fiddle with the ring I was also wearing on a chain.

"I think so." She reached up and unhooked the necklace from around her neck, slipping the ring off before she slid it onto her finger. I followed suit.

A smile curled my lips when I woke the next morning and felt the ring on my finger. After a quick shower and a cup of coffee, I left because I needed to get to the brewery. Her brother was getting in his car nearby, and I resisted the urge to flag him down and demand he let me know when he planned to tell her. I didn't like the weight of carrying his secret.

Chapter Twenty-Four

ROSIE

The light from above glinted on my wedding band, drawing my eyes to it. Almost every time I noticed it was on my hand, I internally started, followed by a softness in my heart.

I loved Wyatt. Of that, I had no doubt. I told myself all the things I thought I should. That being anxious about commitment was normal for anyone. Even for someone whose mother had died in a startling way. I told myself it was worth the risk. That Wyatt was worth it all.

So when my worst nightmare happened when I was on shift at the hospital, I told myself it was just pure coincidence. It had nothing to do with my conversation with Wyatt about my mother. I feared his faith in me and my ability to keep it cool during an emergency might've been misplaced.

When a woman gave birth and we couldn't get the bleeding to stop, it was all hands-on deck. I couldn't help but think of my mother and what that night must've been like for her. The mother was in her thirties, just like mine had been. This was her second child, and the labor seemed to go fairly smoothly, although her OB-GYN had been monitoring her in the past week due to concerns about bleeding.

She got to hold her little baby boy, who they named Danny. As the nurses began going through the usual steps after the baby was born, the bleeding wasn't slowing. At all. She began to look scared when her breathing became labored, and it was clear she was weakening.

With modern medicine, it was easy to trick yourself into thinking we could handle anything. We certainly could handle many things, far more than in earlier times. Yet childbirth was always risky. A multitude of factors were at play, but the data started to point us to a serious problem. Her blood pressure was plummeting, nothing we did could bring it up, and multiple doctors began filling the room.

"What's happening?" Her voice was shaky. Giving birth stretches a body to its limit.

I ran in and out of the room, sending people to check on our blood supply and making sure we called for more if needed. I obviously hadn't been there when this happened to my mother, but the old memories were fresh at this moment. The hospital staff allowed us in to see her, and I remembered a sense of panic setting in when we were escorted out later. I hadn't understood what was happening but knew it was serious. I had felt the somber tone of the room. It took my mother approximately twenty-four hours to essentially bleed to death.

I wished I had never looked at her records. Before the ability to give people blood transfusions to keep them alive, literally, she would've died much more quickly. There would've been no way to even hope she could've made it.

My mind was jolted back to the moment when one of the ER doctors, Dr. Jackson, spoke my name. His voice was calm and low like it always was. He was older, and he only worked part-time now. He said he liked to do the ER shift because it helped keep him on his toes. He said it was an injection of vitality because he remembered just how much life meant.

When he approached me, I was in the break room with my elbows on my knees, fighting the exhaustion setting in. I didn't even know how many hours I'd been at the hospital.

I glanced up with blurry eyes to see him standing in the doorway. "Cassie is going to make it. She's finally stabilized," Dr. Jackson said.

I burst into tears. He walked across the room and sat down on the bench beside me, his big hand landing between my shoulder blades. He moved it in a slow circle. His touch alone was soothing. He was a big man, easily a few inches over six feet tall. Nothing seemed to rattle him. Until tonight, I'd thought nothing rattled me at work.

"Breathe, Rosie."

I took several slow breaths. After a few moments, my tears had stopped, and I could straighten up. I glanced over at him, feeling sheepish. "I'm sorry," I said quickly.

"You don't need to apologize. We all have those cases. For some, they're few and far between. I understand why it's happening for you. I wasn't the doctor who treated your mother, but I was on duty that night. I remember how everyone felt. It was a long night, and, unlike Cassie, she didn't make it. I'm not telling you anything you don't know, but there's always a risk in life. Some of those risks are very close to our hearts. I want you to go home to your new husband." His eyes twinkled a little at that. He had teased me about my Vegas wedding the other day. "And remember to tell him you love him. Are you okay?"

Whenever Dr. Jackson asked that question, it was always slow and with purpose. You could tell he really wanted to know if you were actually okay.

I nodded slowly. "I'm okay."

He moved his hand in one more slow circle before he held it in place and gave me a light pat, almost as if to emphasize my answer. "You are okay. It might help to pop in and check on Cassie before you leave tonight."

After Dr. Jackson left the break room, I remained seated for another few minutes. I did an internal body check. I felt tired and weary in a way that wasn't typical for me. I was just exhausted, sucked dry from the emotion of trying to help keep someone alive. That was difficult, no matter what. But to have it be something that had actually led to my mother's death was something else altogether. I let out a sharp breath. Tonight's events had taken me by surprise, resurrecting a grief I thought had passed.

If I'd learned one thing in all the years since I'd lost my mother, it was that you truly could not change the past. There were no do-overs. All you could do was try to find a way forward through the pain. Over time, the loss did become smaller, except you were always carrying it in your heart. Sometimes the pain of it was sharp, like when you hit your funny bone on something. It reverberated like an electrical shock, unexpected and piercing enough to take your breath away.

I swallowed and gulped in a breath of air before I stood. A few moments later, I took Dr. Jackson's advice and stopped in to see how Cassie was doing. I was a professional, and this was my job. Even if tonight's events had hit startlingly close to home, preparing yourself for the life-and-death moments we faced daily was always a challenge.

I was so profoundly relieved Cassie had made it through, that modern medicine helped turn the tide. It wasn't as if I thought our team had completely saved her. It was a combination of details: her body responding in the right way at the right time and her having just enough reserves in her system to make it through a dicey situation.

When I walked into her room, she was propped up in bed, holding her newborn son. Her husband was in a chair beside the bed, sound asleep. I knew he had been awake for much of this, trying to be there for her the whole time.

Cassie had a weary and deeply felt smile on her face. My hands were actually shaking a little. This was the moment that my mother never got. I had to blink away the tears stinging my eyes.

I almost didn't trust myself to touch her. Typically, I might've rested a hand on a patient's shoulder. In this case, I started by lightly curling my palm around the back of her baby's head. "He looks great. So do you." I was relieved my voice was steady.

Her smile softened as she let out a sigh. "Thank you. I still remember your voice telling me to hold on. I tried. Thank you so much. I don't know what happened, but I'm glad to be here now."

I tipped my head to the side and felt my strength rolling in along with the calm I had called upon time and again. "We can explain it later when you're feeling a little better. For now, you're okay, and that's all that matters."

She blinked up at me. Her son was sound asleep on her chest.

"I'm done with my shift, so I'm heading out. They'll keep you for a few days to make sure you're stable. I'll check in on you tomorrow, okay?"

Cassie nodded, her eyes sliding over toward her husband. "I think he's tired."

I laughed softly. "I'm not sure how much you remember, but he was with you for most of it."

"I know he was." Tears glittered in her eyes. "Thank you again."

As I left, all I could think was that I needed to see Wyatt. It was a near desperate feeling to be in his presence.

I texted him before I drove away.

Me: *I need you tonight.*

Later, I would realize how raw and vulnerable it was for me to write that.

Chapter Twenty-Five

ROSIE

Wyatt: *On my way.*

When I got home, Wyatt's car was already there. My emotions felt right there on the edge. Everything felt raw as if my nerves were exposed to the air. I needed him, needed the comfort of his presence, the warmth of his embrace, and the way I felt protected and safe with him.

We were comfortable enough now and in enough of a pattern that he was already inside the house. When I walked through the door, he stood by the kitchen counter. My eyes absorbed a few details—his jacket hanging on the hook by the door, his boots in the shoe tray, one of them tipped over. That detail was somehow comforting because one of his boots was always tipped over, specifically the right one because he kicked it off second.

He turned toward the door. He wore navy blue socks, a pair of jeans, and a navy T-shirt that brought out the blue of his eyes. His gaze met mine. I had no idea what he saw on my face, but he crossed to me quickly, helping me slide my jacket off and hanging it up as I slipped out of my shoes. Without a word, he folded me in his arms. I tucked my head into his chest, breathing in his familiar scent.

I didn't even realize I was crying until I heard him saying, "Hey, hey, it's okay, Rosie. It's okay."

I trembled all over as the emotions discharged from my system. He simply held me, not demanding to know what happened, just comforting me and holding me. I had no idea how much time had passed before my tears slowed, and I could breathe.

I took in another gulp of his scent before I lifted my head. I could smell the hint of detergent in his T-shirt and the mingled scents from the brewery and him underneath it all. He smoothed my hair away from my cheek with one hand, holding me firm in his arms as he asked, "Sweetheart, what happened?"

I took a shaky breath and surprised myself completely by simply answering honestly. "We had to treat a woman who went through exactly what happened to my mom. She survived, but it was terrifying, and it just brought up—" My words ran out abruptly. I circled my hand in the air. "So many things. I'm exhausted."

"Are you okay?" Wyatt pressed a kiss to my forehead.

"Yeah. It just caught me off guard."

"I bet it did. But you're okay, and it sounds like she's okay. What do you need? We can get you in the shower. I brought pizza with me. It's warming in the oven. Tell me what you need."

As if my body knew, my stomach growled in response. "Pizza would be perfect."

Chapter Twenty-Six

WYATT

The light in Rosie's bedroom was low, cast from a single lamp beside her bed. Her hair tangled around her shoulders. Her skin was dewy, and her eyes wide and dark.

One of my hands gripped her at the hip, my fingers pressing into her skin. She rocked with me. I felt as if I was exactly where I belonged.

My need rushed through me like a storm with gale-force winds. My release threatened, my balls tightening as I clung to my control, savoring the indescribable pleasure of being sheathed inside her. She rippled around me. My heart kicked along, and it felt as if it were about to crack one of my ribs.

There was sex, and there was what we had—this intense, wild mixture of fierce lust laced within deep emotion and intimacy. It felt as if it transcended love. This was how it always was when I was with her.

"Come with me," I whispered.

She blinked just as she rose and sank down again. I knew her body's call. She began to tremble, and I slid my other hand up her back, pressing between her shoulder blades to pull her closer. I brought my lips to hers, catching her cry just as she came, shuddering all over.

I finally let go, the line of my control breaking loose as my release jolted through me. A few moments later, she curled against me, and I held her close. Tonight had been one moment after another. Rosie felt tender and vulnerable in a way that was rare for her. I would've just held her tonight, but she wanted this. She'd said, "I need you now."

When Rosie needed me, I would do my best to give her whatever she needed.

A little while later, we untangled ourselves, and she shimmied close to me after I turned out the light. The last thing I remembered was her pressing a kiss at the base of my throat just before she tucked her head into the curve of my neck and letting out a soft sigh.

Her brother texted her the following morning, saying he wanted us to meet him and their dad at Spill the Beans Café. I was too caught up in how good it felt to be with Rosie to start worrying yet.

———

It all felt so uneventful at first. We got coffee, and Rosie held my hand. I didn't even know how to explain the warm sense of joy I felt, just having it open to the world that we were together. Rosie's dad clapped me on the shoulder as we walked over to the table with him.

Only after I'd had two swallows of coffee did I realize there might be a problem.

Rosie's brother looked over at her nervously and

then at me. The guy didn't even lead into what he said. "Rosie, I went to rehab. I'm in recovery. I'm doing fine. I just need you to know that's what happened."

Rosie blinked, lowering the mug she'd been lifting to the table. "What?" She looked bewildered, and I slid my arm around her shoulders.

It all went straight to hell from there.

"He's doing good, Rosie, real good," her dad said.

"You knew?" she squeaked.

Her dad nodded. "I haven't known for long, though."

The tension building inside me was tight like a band squeezing around my chest.

Rosie's face was pale, and she gripped her mug with both hands. She glanced from her brother to her dad and finally to me. She read right through me.

"You knew?" she pressed, anger and betrayal flicking in her eyes.

"I found out by accident. Brent told me he was going to tell you," I said quickly.

Her brother seemed to realize we were in dicey territory here. Rosie looked around the table again. "I'm not upset that you were in rehab. I understand. You didn't have to tell me, but why does everybody know but me? Why is it a secret only from me? Did I do something to make you think I might judge you for this?"

"No, Rosie, no," her brother said quickly. "I'm just —oh, fuck." He let out a ragged sigh, running his hands through his hair. "The only reason Wyatt knows is he saw me coming out of an NA meeting in the basement at Fireweed Industries. As soon as he saw me, I knew he knew something was up. I just told him because I didn't want to have to lie. I was planning to tell you at some point, so I asked him to give me a chance to tell you. Don't hold anything against him."

Rosie looked utterly stricken. "Why is it a secret from me? I hate secrets."

Before I could get another word out, she jumped up from the table and started to hurry out. The soles of her shoes squeaked on the floor when she stopped abruptly and turned back. "I love you, all of you." She looked at her brother. "I'm glad you're okay, and I'm really proud of you. I know recovery is really hard. I just wish—" She swallowed. "I don't know what I did, but I guess you don't feel like you can tell me things unless you have to. I'm sorry."

Then she was gone, practically running out of the café. We'd driven here separately because she had to go to work. I hurried out behind her. "Rosie!"

She stopped at her car. "It's okay, Wyatt. I understand."

"Rosie." I took another step closer to where she stood by her car door.

Her gaze was carefully blank. "You don't need to apologize. I just need some time."

"I love you," I said.

She stared at me. "I love you too, but I still need time." She climbed in her car and drove away, and it was all I could do not to follow her.

"She definitely needs some time." Her father's gruff voice came from behind me.

I turned back to find him standing nearby. "She hates feeling like she doesn't know what's going on, which I suppose most people do."

I scuffed the toe of my boot on the gravel. "I didn't even want to know this," I muttered, throwing my hands up and letting them fall.

"Of course you didn't. And it was her brother's

story to tell. I kind of think I should've handled things better when her mom died. She was at the hospital, and I knew it didn't look good for her mom, but I kept telling Rosie it would be okay. It wasn't, and later, she felt like I kept that from her. Then I was a single dad with a baby. I did my best to handle as much as I could by myself, but she stepped in a lot. Brent looks up to her like a mom. He's always worried he's going to let her down. She understands it wasn't your secret. Just give her a minute."

"It's been a minute," I pointed out. My throat ached.

Her father smiled wryly. A moment later, he tugged me into a one-armed embrace. I could feel the unsteadiness on his feet as I hugged him in return.

I understood why Rosie worried about her father. She worried about him, she worried about her brother, and now she felt like everybody kept a secret from her.

"Can you tell me how long a minute is for the purposes of this situation?" I stepped back, trying to make light of it, but it hurt like fucking hell.

Chapter Twenty-Seven

ROSIE

One week later

There was a knock on my door, and I eyed it skeptically. People didn't usually just stop by my house. In fact, the list of anyone who might, was short. My dad, my brother, Wyatt, or maybe one of my close friends.

"I know you're in there, Rosie." My dad's voice was muted through the door.

I finished rinsing a plate in the sink before I tucked it in the dishwasher and snagged a towel as I walked over to the door.

I was still drying my hands when I opened it. "Hey, Dad."

"Hey." He stood there and swayed a little on his feet.

And, dammit, I knew he was okay for the most part, but his unsteadiness on his feet made my chest ache. I wanted to be mad at him. My heart was still a little broken over how everybody knew the whole truth but me.

Without thinking, I reached for his other hand and guided him inside. "Dad, you could've texted me. I would've walked over there. I don't like you walking on the path over here. It's not level," I scolded him.

He glanced up at me once I had him seated in the kitchen. "It's good for me to move around. The worst thing that can happen is I fall," he pointed out, his smile wry and a little mischievous.

I glared at him. "I don't want you to fall! What if you break something?"

He rolled his eyes. "I walked real slow, and I got my cane." He tapped it on the floor before propping it against the wall where the edge of the counter met it. "Enough about that. How are you doing?"

I crossed over to the coffee pot. "Fine. Would you like some coffee?"

"Already had some this morning. Why don't you give your husband a call? I'm sure he might like some."

It felt as if he'd just dragged a knife over the surface of my heart. It was sore and throbbing. It was the kind of pain that made you wince if you thought about it. I needed to button myself back up, and guard myself against being stupid again.

"Dad, I'll talk to Wyatt when I'm ready."

"Have you talked to your brother?"

As if my father had conjured my little brother, there was another sharp knock on my door, and Brent's voice immediately followed. "I know you're in there with Dad, Rosie. Can I come in?"

I gave my dad a sideways glare as I called out, "Come on in!"

Brent walked in, his eyes bouncing from our father

to me and back again. "What's going on? Are we having coffee, and I didn't get an invite?"

I gestured to the empty stool at the counter. Brent walked over with his long, rangy stride. He'd always been such a skinny kid, and he still was. Maybe someday he'd fill out a little, but I wasn't too sure about that.

"Have you talked to Wyatt?" Brent asked.

I narrowed my eyes at him. "I see we're wasting no time with polite conversation. You could start with the weather," I pointed out, unable to keep the sharpness and hurt out of my tone.

Brent didn't even address that comment. "Wyatt wanted to tell you right off, but I asked him to give me a chance to tell you first." My brother rested his elbows on the counter, dropping his head down as he ran both hands through his hair before straightening and flattening his palms on the table. "Rosie, you are one of the most important people in my life. I know you're not my mother, but you kind of are to me." He glanced quickly at our father. "I know you did your best to make sure it didn't feel like that, but she's eight years older than me. Mom died the day after I was born. I think sometimes life is messy. You didn't ask her to be like a mom to me, but it was just a situation."

It was all I could do not to burst into tears. "Brent, you don't have to explain. You didn't even have to tell me you went to rehab."

"But I want to explain. I *want* to tell you. College was a shit show for me. My grades weren't good, and it was just hard for me. I got in with the wrong crowd. I was having a little too much fun, and that was plain stupid. I got hooked on painkillers. Those things are like freaking candy on college campuses." He paused, closing his eyes as he let out a weary sigh.

"I know they are," I said softly. "They're wildly addictive. Those pharmaceutical companies should burn in hell for lying and insisting they weren't addictive before it was too late. They're everywhere now. Trust me, I work at the hospital. I know how bad it is." My cheeks puffed out with a deep sigh. "Brent..." I began.

My brother looked up, holding my gaze. I realized I'd almost launched into telling him how much I worried about him and all of those things. Yet he had gone to rehab. He had done the hard part, and he was still doing it. "I'm sorry I made it hard to tell me," I finally said.

"You didn't. I just didn't want to worry you. I didn't want to disappoint you. I wasn't worried that you would judge me. Never."

"Are you sure?"

"Absolutely. If you're worried about Dad keeping the secret from you, I only told him last week too. After I ran into Wyatt coming out of the NA meeting, I figured I needed to be open with everyone."

My eyes stung, but I managed not to cry. My chest felt so tight, and I was constantly worried, worried, worried.

My dad leaned over, curling his arm around my shoulders. "Rosie girl, I know you worry a lot. Your brother's got this. He has to do this himself."

"I know," I whispered.

My brother rounded the counter to pull me into a big hug. He was a good hugger. A funny moment flashed through my mind. When he was a toddler, he used to run straight for me and fling his arms around my legs. He was now a good foot taller than me and holding me strong and sure.

When he stepped back, I could see the tears glistening in his eyes. "I love you, sis."

"I love you too." I took a slow breath. "You're gonna make me cry."

"It's okay to cry."

A few tears rolled down my cheeks. I blew my nose with a napkin. I leaned back before I took a gulp of my coffee.

"About Wyatt," my brother began.

"I'll talk to him. I will," I insisted.

"When I asked him to give me time to tell you, the look on his face was one of actual pain," Brent said. "I swear."

I swallowed. "I'm sure it was."

"That man loves you. I can tell," Brent said.

"It's plain as day," my dad said bluntly. "And I speak from experience." My dad's eyes slid to my brother. "Not that I'm doubting you, but you're only—"

"Twenty-two," my brother offered. "I might be young, but I've been through some shit. I know love when I see it."

We laughed together, but my heart twisted a little. Anxiety tightened around my chest. My brother *had* been through some shit.

As if he could read my mind, his gaze sobered before he added, "I know that because you are a nurse and deal with addicts rolling through the ER, you're going to worry. Just so you know, it was short-lived for me. My doctor tells me I'm lucky. I'm young, and I'm resilient. I realized I was in trouble pretty quickly and went to get help. I lucked out and got a really good counselor at the college campus, and he immediately referred me to rehab." My brother shook his head a little. "I'm good. I'm working my ass off. I'm gonna be okay. I let Dad know when I told him last week that I do want to take over the hardware store, but not until I'm a little further into my recovery. That's a lot of responsibility, so I don't want to do it until I'm ready."

I was surprised the inside of my cheeks didn't bleed from holding back. I wanted to offer all kinds of suggestions, but I had to let this one go. I had to let my brother figure it out. I took a deep breath, letting it out in a gust. "You'll figure it out when you're ready. And only if that's what you want to do, right?" I glanced at my dad.

He nodded firmly. "Absolutely. We'll do it when you're ready, no sooner. If you change your mind, that's fine."

Brent looked between us. "Thank you both for being here for me."

"Always," I replied.

My father's sharp gaze arced to me. "So when do you plan to talk to Wyatt?"

Chapter Twenty-Eight

ROSIE

"Oh wow, that's a lot," Tessa said.

McKenna sat beside me and curled her arm around my shoulders, squeezing hard before leaning back in her chair. We were having one of our get-togethers. It happened to be the evening after my brother told me everything, and I was filling them in.

So far, it was me, Tessa, McKenna, and Haven. Fiona was on her way, but she was running late. We were at Tessa's new house, the one she'd moved into with Adam.

"Have you talked to Wyatt yet?" Haven piped up as she returned to the table, setting a stack of pizza boxes in the center.

"Thank God, this is a big table," McKenna teased as she set the pizza boxes in a row in the center.

Tessa began passing out plates and napkins.

"No, I haven't talked to him yet. Well, maybe my brother did. I'm not so sure they're not talking to him every day and keeping him up to speed on my life," I said dryly.

Haven let out a soft laugh. "Maybe. I doubt it, though."

"Your dad, but probably not your brother," McKenna interjected. "I adore your dad, and he can't help but worry about you."

I let out a small sigh. "I'll talk to Wyatt. It's just been a lot to deal with."

Just then, Fiona arrived. After the brief commotion of greetings and starting to eat, the conversation circled back to me, unfortunately.

"Do we have to talk about me?" I asked as soon as Fiona mentioned she'd seen Wyatt that day at the restaurant.

Fiona's eyes slid to mine. "Well, we don't have to, but the poor guy looks brokenhearted. I'm serious. It's kind of sad."

McKenna pressed her lips together to keep from laughing.

"Is that funny?" I couldn't help but interject, suddenly feeling protective of Wyatt.

"Oh, now it's getting to you," Tessa teased lightly.

I tried to chew my feelings away with a vigorous bite of pizza.

Fiona set her slice of pizza down and glanced toward me. "Wyatt wanted to tell you. Your brother asked him to give him a chance to tell you. Considering how sensitive issues are around substance abuse, I think it would've been awkward for Wyatt to tell you without your brother being okay with it. It's a seriously touchy subject."

Pain twisted in my chest. "I know, I know. It's just..."

The next thing I knew, I was telling my friends the whole story of how emotionally raw I'd felt after the situation at the hospital and how it brought up so many feelings about my mother. I was surprised that I didn't just break down in tears and fall apart.

While they all knew my mom had died when I was little, none of them had known the details about what happened. When I finished explaining, McKenna looked over at me with tears shining in her eyes. "I knew that your mom died when she gave birth to your brother, but I didn't know how it happened. I'm so sorry." She was sitting beside me and leaned close, curling her arm around my shoulders and squeezing tight for a moment.

McKenna and I had bonded when we were younger through a shared, silent understanding of what it meant to lose a parent you loved. She had been some years younger than me when her father died, but she understood what it meant. Like those days in school, they would assign a project to make something for Mother's Day or Father's Day. We were the ones who didn't have anything to make for one of the days. No one meant to hurt others when those things happened. It was just part of life. You learned to deal with the jagged edge of the pain that came up in those moments.

"So that happened, and then you found out what your brother's been dealing with. That's a lot," Tessa said softly.

I swallowed through the tightness in my throat. "It's been a rough patch."

I got some much-needed understanding and a few hugs.

"What do you want?" Fiona's question was soft.

"What do you mean?" I asked.

"With Wyatt," she clarified.

Her question sent me spiraling inside. For a second, my mind tried to take hold of the reins, but my heart kicked hard and fast, zooming past it. My heart *knew* I loved Wyatt.

I took an unsteady breath. My lips twisted to the side, and I felt a little sheepish as I looked around at my friends. "Well, I mean, we're married," I began slowly.

McKenna tipped her head to the side. "You are, and somehow, you kept it a secret from everybody but Rhys."

"Rhys told you what he saw?" I glanced toward Haven.

She hitched her brows up. "He did. We chalked it up to you and Wyatt being drunk. I was positive you didn't actually get married. I kept telling him there was no way you really went through with it. He swore me to secrecy, and I didn't dwell on it since I didn't think it was real. None of us knew about your other thing, though."

"What other thing?" Fiona interjected.

Heat flashed into my cheeks. "Right before I went to nursing school, uh, Wyatt and I kind of had a fling."

"And nobody knew?" Fiona squeaked.

I shook my head quickly. "Not everybody was in town. McKenna was already living in Seattle and—" I glanced toward Tessa. "Where were you?"

"Dating my asshole of an ex and trying to avoid everyone because I was miserable," she said flatly. "I wasn't paying attention to much of anything at that point."

I took a deep breath and let it out in a gusty sigh. "I am *so* glad you divorced him."

She nodded before a slow smile unfurled across her face. "I am too."

Tessa's ex had been abusive, but now she was very happily in love with Adam. She deserved every bit of goodness she got after what she'd gone through.

Fiona was determined to keep this conversation on track. "So no one knew you had a fling with Wyatt before you went to nursing school, and you never got over him?"

I bit my lip to keep from laughing. "I don't know if I would put it that way. It was a really great week, but we were young, and he was leaving to be a firefighter. I was headed straight to nursing school. Even though it was amazing, we didn't, or I just didn't think anything would come of it. He has always been the most memorable. Not that I dated much because I didn't. Dating is annoying. Dating apps are hell—mostly dick pics and obnoxious guys who don't want any commitment. In a funny way, minus the dick pics and being obnoxious, that's what I had with Wyatt back then—no commitment and a week of great benefits. In hindsight, it didn't feel like that. It felt like more, but off to school I went. I didn't think about it much since he wasn't living here when I moved back to town. Then we were in Vegas and—" My cheeks were on fire, and I shrugged because I didn't know what else to say.

McKenna nudged me with her knee, and I glanced over at her. "What?"

"Wyatt loves you, and he's sad. Please put him out of his misery," she said, her words solemn.

Chapter Twenty-Nine

WYATT

"Get your head out of your ass," Griffin said bluntly.

"I think we might have to yank it out," Blake chimed in.

We were in the break room at the restaurant and brewery, seated at the big round table in the back corner. Blake had told us to stop by because Fiona was testing recipes. I glanced between my brothers and rolled my eyes. "Where are those samples? I'm freaking starving."

"Right here!" Fiona's voice reached us as she walked into the room with a large tray propped on her shoulder.

Blake stood swiftly from the table, striding over and taking the tray from her. "I told you not to carry so much."

Fiona looked at her husband, pressing her lips together to keep from laughing. "I carry trays every day at work. I can handle it."

Blake grumbled something under his breath as he carried the tray over and set it in the center of the table. As Griffin and I began to select options from the samples, the back door opened, and Rhys, Adam, and Kenan came walking in.

"Whoa, it's a full house," Kenan teased.

My brothers snagged chairs at the table. Fiona interjected and clapped her hands together. "Guys!"

I was lifting a bite of something to my mouth and lowered it. "What is it?"

She handed out little sheets of paper, all of which listed the various items we were sampling. "Please just make a note of your favorites. I don't expect too much, but a little something about why you like it would be helpful."

"Are you redoing the menu?" Griffin asked.

"Yes and no. We're always trying to add new specials. I want to test them with you guys first. We're also doing some more events, so I want to expand our catering options as well." She gestured to the tray. "Read the tags so you know what you're trying," she added.

We dutifully began paying attention. Nothing but moans and appreciative murmurs filled the air for a few minutes. Blake caught Fiona by the hand as she turned to leave. "Everything's amazing. I love you," he said.

Her cheeks went pink when he lifted her hand and dropped a kiss on the inside of her wrist. Rhys watched with a smile as Blake's gaze trailed after Fiona when she left the room.

"Dude, you are seriously whipped," Kenan observed.

Blake was utterly unabashed and simply shrugged. "I love Fiona. She's my favorite person. Period." He glanced at me. "When are you planning to wise up and do something about Rosie?"

I took a swallow of water after I finished chewing a

bite of an absolutely amazing cheese-filled pastry. Glancing around after I swallowed, I replied, "She's the one who dumped me."

"Did she actually dump you?" Rhys asked.

I shifted my shoulders. I'd been fighting a headache ever since the morning Rosie drove away and left me behind in the parking lot at Spill the Beans Café. The tension bundled between my shoulder blades was getting worse by the day. "I don't know. She told me she needed some time. Her dad told me to give her some space and that she would come around. So I'm trying to do that. What else am I supposed to do?"

"How long has it been?" Kenan asked.

"Almost two weeks," I muttered. Resting my elbows on the table, I dipped my head down and ran my hands through my hair before I straightened and leaned back in my chair. "I don't know what the fuck to do. Most of you are in love. Tell me what to do to make it right." I gestured around the table.

Everyone's voices crossed over each other, ranging from "Call her" to "Give her space" to "Stop being an idiot."

That last one was from Griffin. I slid my gaze to him. "How am I being an idiot? I think I'm being pretty respectful. Rosie asked for space, and I'm giving it to her."

He nodded. "You're a respectful guy. You can still give her space and maybe just send her a text and say something along the lines of I love you, and I'm here for you when you're ready."

I glanced at Rhys, the oldest brother and the one I'd always thought had all the answers since I was a little kid. "What do you think?"

Rhys took a bite of one of the dessert pastries, a

powdered sugar puffball. He jotted a note before answering, "I think you need to give her space, but Griffin might have a point."

"How am I supposed to give her space and not pressure her if I text her?" I was exasperated.

Rhys let out a put-upon sigh as if he couldn't believe I didn't understand. "You leave her a message, or you send her a text, but don't do anything else for now. She can't ignore you forever. I mean, you *are* married, so unless she flees town and never comes back, she's gonna have to see you, even if it's to file paperwork for divorce."

The stricken way I felt inside must've shown on my face. Griffin angled his head to the side, biting his cheek to keep from laughing. "Okay, it's not funny, but oh, my God, you are so in love with her. Rosie is not going to divorce you. That's totally not a Rosie move. Her father is here, her brothers here, and her husband is here."

"That would be you," Adam interjected dry. "It's going to be fine."

"It is," Blake offered. "But you have to get through the hard part."

"Life is much less complicated when I'm not in love," I said.

"Yeah, but love is worth the pain." Adam clapped me on the shoulder. "You got this."

Chapter Thirty

WYATT

I did not, in fact, have this. I felt like I was walking a tightrope across a chasm growing wider by the day. I didn't know how to get to the other side to where Rosie was.

I didn't want her to think I wasn't willing to fight for her, to fight for us. But I was afraid of pushing her too hard and too fast. We had actually talked about how that week before she went to nursing school and before I flew out into the wilderness to fight fires had been this capsule of time when all the pressure was off because of our circumstances.

I think my heart knew then what my mind wasn't ready for. Maybe I didn't understand love then, but my heart knew there was a possibility with her that I had never experienced before.

I'd kept my distance ever since we'd both landed back in town full-time. Because, damn, Rosie had her guard up, big time.

While I was busy trying to formulate how I was going to talk to her, I stopped to get coffee at Spill the

Beans Café. Both Phyllis and Hazel were there. There was a lull in the crowd since it was late morning.

Phyllis was prepping my coffee while Hazel was refilling the pastry case with a fresh batch of offerings. "You really should try one of these," she said, holding one up.

"Sure, I'll have one." I didn't even know what it was.

I was being polite, and I was a little hungry, but my lack of enthusiasm caused Hazel to straighten and eye me skeptically. "What's wrong?"

I started to hedge before Phyllis tapped a button on the espresso machine and glanced over. "Wyatt and his wife are going through some things."

"Well, I know that," Hazel replied. She rested a hand on her hip and wagged the pastry at me. "You're married. A part of marriage means you'll have your ups and downs, and you have to deal with the hard stuff. That "for better or for worse" thing really means something even if you got married when you were drunk in Las Vegas."

I felt my cheeks get warm and smiled sheepishly between them. "Rosie said she needed space."

"That's your line, and you're sticking to it, huh?" Phyllis said as she rested her hips on the counter and faced me.

"What do you mean 'that's my line'?"

"That's what Griffin mentioned," Hazel piped up.

"And Rhys," Phyllis added.

"And Adam," Hazel said.

"Oh, my God," I muttered. "My brothers are gossiping about me."

Phyllis's brows hitched up. "No, they're not. They were talking to each other. We just heard the whole conversation because they were sitting right over there." She gestured to the table closest to the register.

"They would never gossip and betray you like that," Hazel said.

"Well, I could use another perspective," I finally said.

Hazel and Phyllis both perked up. "What can we tell you?" Hazel asked.

"We were both married to our husbands until death did us part," Phyllis said.

"I'm assuming you know the whole story about me and Rosie?" I prompted.

"That you and Rosie secretly got married in Vegas and didn't tell anybody, but Rhys suspected all along, and then you started a spouses-with-benefits arrangement," Hazel said succinctly.

"And then, you found out Rosie's brother was in recovery by accident. He asked you to give him a chance to tell Rosie himself, which is an honorable thing to do. I give him lots of credit for being in recovery, but wow, dumb move on his part. He should've told her that same day. When he finally told her, Rosie felt that everybody had been hiding it from her. Are we up to speed?" Phyllis asked.

"Wow." I shook my head slowly. "I always figured you knew just about everything going on, but you really do stay on top of it."

"We don't gossip. People just tell us things. Like we're talking to you about this." Hazel angled her head to the side. "But we're not talking about this to anybody else."

"I'm sure we don't know the whole story," Phyllis added.

"You know, Rosie's had to deal with some difficult things in life," I said.

"Of course, she has." Hazel's tone softened. "Her mother died when she was a little girl. Her dad did the best he could, but no matter what, that was a huge loss. The way her brother looks up to her is just..." Hazel pressed her hand to her heart. "It's the sweetest thing, and I'm sure he was afraid he'd let her down. We're so proud of him."

"Did you know Rosie's mom?" I asked.

"Of course we knew her! She was a sweet woman," Hazel said.

"I know you understand loss," Phyllis offered. "When you lost your dad, you know what it does to a person."

So I did. Dad dying had sent our mom into a spiral of grief. To this day, I knew that she wished she could go back and change the way things played out in the years that followed. Our parents had wanted a big family. The downside to that was our mom was pretty overwhelmed after our dad died. On the upside, we all had each other, and I wouldn't trade that for a minute. Our father's death had set into motion a chain of events that led to a lot of pain in our family.

All of this passed through my thoughts before I replied, "I do understand. I'm just trying to figure out what to do now."

I ended up summarizing Griffin's suggestion. Phyllis and Hazel seemed to agree I should reach out in some way. "You could consider a big gesture, but that might be pushy since she wanted space," Hazel said.

"Think of something small that would mean a lot to her," Phyllis suggested.

After my conversation with them, I took my coffee and walked down the street to the brewery. Before I could overthink it, I slipped my phone out of my pocket. With coffee in one hand and my phone in the other, I began typing a text to Rosie.

Me: *I want to give you space because you asked for it. But I also want you to know I love you. That's it.*

I didn't even know if I had hit send before I heard a loud, screeching sound, and everything went black.

Chapter Thirty-One

ROSIE

I reread Wyatt's message with tears welling in my eyes. On the heels of a shaky breath, I tapped out a reply.

Me: *I did ask for space, and you gave me plenty. Honestly, I owe you an apology. The whole thing hurt that day, and it was a lot. I know my brother put you in a bad spot. I love you, and I miss you. Let's make this official-official.* 💍

I found the wedding ring emoticon and smiled to myself when I hit send. I had just arrived at work when his text came in. I set my phone in my locker and quickly changed into my scrubs, then checked it once more before I hopped into the shift. I tried not to be let down that he hadn't responded yet.

I was heading down the hallway to the nurses' station. It was a big circular desk with hallways branching off. I heard the sound of a siren departing the hospital as I pushed through the swinging door into the desk area. "What's our status?"

The last ER supervisor quickly updated me on the status of the most recent patients who'd been admitted. One had come in with chest pains, and another after a severe asthma attack when they ran out of inhalers because their insurance wouldn't pay for them.

I met Linda's gaze. "In the next life, can we have some type of gladiator ring where we all get to put the insurance company people in the middle?" I let out a sharp sigh. "This is life and death for her. She's had asthma since she was a little girl."

Linda pressed her lips together. "I know. Sign me up. Onto the next, we have a new kid, just diagnosed with type one diabetes. He's fighting his parents on his insulin shots. He should be ready for discharge soon. That call we just heard? Somebody got hit by a motorcycle on Main Street. Both the motorcyclist and the pedestrian were injured. I'm gonna get the hell out of here before they get back with that one. We have a full crew, and Dr. Jackson is on duty today, so you are in the best hands."

I waved her off. I knew I only had a short window before the ambulance got back, so I zipped around to check on everyone. For a brief few minutes, it was quiet. That never lasted in an emergency room, but you took the moments when you got them. I was walking back down the hallway when I heard the doors to the emergency bay opening. The EMT crew came in, racing down the hallway with two stretchers.

I was checking on the guy driving the motorcycle when I glanced over my shoulder and realized the man he'd hit was Wyatt. My stomach plummeted to my feet, and my heart felt like it might literally fall out of my chest. I froze, just as I had been about to move to put the IV needle in the man's wrist.

"Rosie!" one of the EMTs said.

I glanced over, and he must've seen the look on my face. "I got it," he said swiftly.

My hands were shaking as he took the IV needle from me. I knew what I should do was turn and walk straight away. I was trembling all over. But I couldn't. I stepped to the side of Wyatt's stretcher. They already had an oxygen mask on him. My eyes landed on a scrape on his hand, a tear in his jeans, and a small bandage on his forehead.

"What's the status?" If this crew noticed my wobbly voice, it didn't slow them down.

"Unconscious when we arrived. Came to within a minute or so. We've already contacted his family. I assume they'll be here any minute. We did the initial concussion checks, but when we moved him to adjust his leg, which is broken, he passed out from the pain. It's a clean break. We just need to get it set."

"We should do a scan for any internal bleeding," I croaked.

Dr. Jackson appeared at my side. "I'll handle this, Rosie."

"Dr. Jackson, I am—"

He put a hand on my shoulder. "His vitals are stable. We need to set the break."

"I need you to do a scan," I pressed with adrenaline nudging the panicky feeling inside higher and higher. I was on the verge of creating a scene.

"We will. I need you to let me handle this. You can stay on duty, but you need to stay at the desk, or monitor anyone who is currently stable. That's it," he said firmly.

I was frozen in place. Dr. Jackson called a name, and someone appeared at my side and literally led me away from Wyatt.

A while later, I sort of came out of my fog. I was

sitting on a chair inside the nurses' station. Everything else was carrying on around me. The phone was ringing, monitors beeping, and one of the nurses was typing and talking to someone on the phone.

I looked around, catching the eye of Harry, one of the nurses on duty. "He's fine," he said.

"How long has it been since I sat down here?"

He moved his hand back and forth. "Fifteen minutes, give or take. They've had time to do the X-ray and the scan you demanded. Dr. Jackson probably did that just as a favor to you."

Dr. Jackson's voice came from the other side of the desk. "Not as a favor to Rosie. You never know what might happen whenever someone's hit by a moving vehicle. We're going to get him prepped to set the break. He should be done in about an hour. He doesn't need full anesthesia for this, but we're going to sedate him." Dr. Jackson held my eyes as I began to stand. "You are not to come in until he's in the recovery room." With that, he hurried off.

I sat back down. "How's the motorcyclist?" I asked.

Harry replied, "Just a little banged up. He feels terrible. There were some witnesses. Apparently, Wyatt just walked into traffic while texting on his phone."

"Oh my God. Are you serious?"

"That's what the cop said," another nurse chimed in as she spun away from her computer.

"He just texted me right before my shift started. Oh my God," I muttered. I was dumbfounded. "I can't just sit here. I have to do something."

Harry caught me by the elbow as I stood from my chair. "How about you just check on things? Please do not check on Wyatt or the motorcyclist."

I knew he was right on that, but it drove me crazy not to check on Wyatt. It was a relief to have something to focus on, though. I chatted with the parents of the little boy, who was very upset about his diabetes because he hated shots. Our chest pain patient was being monitored, but he likely had a panic attack. Many people confuse those for a heart attack, so that wasn't anything unusual, but a single dose of anxiety medication had eliminated all of his chest pains and distress and his vitals were stable.

I was still distraught and concerned about Wyatt, but I felt a little steadier. I was returning to the nurses' station when I saw Cassie walking in. When her eyes landed on me, she smiled. She had her baby in a little sling across her chest.

She stopped at the desk. "I'm so glad you're here. I wanted to come in and thank everyone. I figured you might not all be on duty, but—" She let out a quick sigh. "I'm doing much better. I feel mostly normal now, and Danny is doing great."

We collectively cooed over the baby, and she delivered us a tray of pastries from Spill the Beans Café. "I figure those are popular anytime," she explained.

I was still restless and needed something to do. I lingered over the baby and walked with Cassie toward the entrance. When we stopped by the doors, she glanced over at me. I didn't know what she saw in my eyes, but she offered, "It'll be okay."

"It will?" My voice lilted up.

"One way or another. By the way, I heard you got married in Vegas." Her eyes twinkled with her smile. "Congratulations."

A few minutes later, Dr. Jackson tapped me on the shoulder where I was organizing our supply room because I was restless. I spun around. "What is it? How is he?"

"Wyatt is stable. It was a clean break. No complications. He's currently sleeping, but you can see him. I think you should officially go off the clock before you do that," he explained.

"But I'm—"

"Going to have coverage for supervision for the shift from the lead nurse," Dr. Jackson interjected. "Go see the man you love."

A few minutes later, I walked into Wyatt's room. The hospital was at capacity, so it wasn't a private room. The man in the other bed was the guy who had a panic attack. He had fallen back asleep since I'd checked on him.

I carefully stepped behind the curtain between the two beds and rounded Wyatt's bed to stand by the window as I rested my hands on the railing. He was still asleep, likely out from the sedative they had given him to set his broken leg. His skin looked pale under the bright lighting. I lifted a hand to smooth away his mussed hair from his forehead. He must've cut his head somehow because I could feel the abraded area on his skin just inside his hairline. It had been cleaned and disinfected.

Emotion rolled up inside, a big, slow wave, catching in a high curl. "I love you," I whispered.

I smoothed one of his eyebrows with my fingertip just as his eyes blinked open. For a moment, he looked confused.

"Rosie?" he croaked.

"Hey," I said quietly. "You got hit by a motorcycle. Do you remember anything?"

Wyatt rolled his head from side to side before bringing his attention to me. "I was texting you." He blinked. "Nothing hurts right now." His lips curled in a kind of loopy smile.

I didn't realize a tear had rolled down my cheek until he tried to reach up and wipe it away. His hand landed on my shoulder instead before bouncing to land on his chest. "Don't cry. I'm fine. Why am I in the hospital?"

"You broke your leg. The motorcyclist got a little bruised up and feels terrible."

"Oh fuck. I wasn't paying attention. So what happened?"

"Apparently, you walked into the street, and the motorcyclist hit you. According to witnesses, he wasn't going very fast, and you just stepped into traffic. Dr. Jackson said it was a clean break. They did a scan, and everything else is good. The only other thing I see is this little scrape on your forehead. I'm sure you'll have some bruising because you can't just land on the pavement and not get a little banged up."

I was trying to keep it together. Really, I was, but I couldn't seem to manage it. The tears kept rolling down my cheeks. Before I knew it, I was hiccupping when I tried to speak.

Wyatt reached up, curling an arm around my waist and trying to pull me closer. "For fuck's sake," he muttered. "Can we get this bed to go up?"

I couldn't talk, but I could do that and tapped the button to raise it. A moment later, I sobbed into his chest. He kept his arm around my waist and held me close. It was only a minute or so before my burst of tears subsided.

I straightened and looked down at him. "How are you feeling?"

"Physically? Like I'm on a big puffy cloud. I can't really feel much of anything," he said.

"Good." I swallowed. "Sorry about that."

"For what?"

I could feel the gentle squeeze of his palm where it rested on the side of my waist.

"I overreacted," I explained.

Because it was Wyatt and he understood me better than myself maybe, he instantly caught up to the fact I wasn't talking about this particular moment.

"You did not overreact. That was a lot to take in. I didn't know what to do. When your brother said he wanted an opportunity to tell you, I thought he would tell you in a day or so. I felt stuck because it wasn't my secret to share."

"I know, and I understand." I leaned up, looking into his eyes. "I love you, Wyatt."

"I love you, and I always will," he said gruffly.

"You sure about that?" I managed to tease as I trailed my fingertips over the prickly stubble of his beard.

"There are a lot of things I'm not sure about, but I am sure about that. I'd break my leg all over again if that's what it takes for this."

"You didn't need to break your leg," I protested. "I was going to talk to you anyway."

"Did you get my text?" he asked.

I nodded. "Did you get my reply?"

He shook his head and promptly demonstrated just how puffy that cloud was. He tried to make some serious moves on me from a freaking hospital bed.

We had to wait a solid two hours before the hospital cleared him for discharge. Various members of his family stopped int to check on him while we waited. I even tried to get bossy and move it along, but there wasn't much I could do. Hospitals were like a tunnel. Once you were in it, you just had to go through it to get to the other side. I was beyond relieved when I could take him home with me.

I stopped by the pharmacy to pick up the medication Dr. Jackson had prescribed for pain.

A few hours later, I was so happy to have Wyatt propped up on pillows in my bed, I was almost giddy from it.

Chapter Thirty-Two

WYATT

"No." Rosie stared at me from the foot of the bed, her arms akimbo. Her expression was implacable. "You can't do that, Wyatt. Every time you put too much weight on that foot, you potentially risk messing up the set. You're a big guy."

"I thought you liked the fact that I'm a big guy," I pointed out.

"I do, but in this case, it means there's more weight to put on it because there's more of you. I will be right back with a cup of coffee and your crutches," she said, her eyes narrowing.

I grinned as I watched her walk briskly out of the bedroom. A moment later, she returned.

She handed me a mug of coffee and held out my pain medication.

I shook my head. "You can make me use crutches, but I'm done with that pain medication. It makes me feel tired and out of it. Dr. Jackson said I could try alternating ibuprofen and acetaminophen instead."

Rosie pressed her lips together. "Wyatt—"

I reached for her hand and reeled her close to me. When her knees hit the edge of the mattress, I gave a tug, and she tumbled half across me. "Wyatt!"

"Sweetheart, I'm fine. In fact..." I rocked my hips up into her. Her belly had landed right across *that* part of me.

Her eyes widened.

"I'll be in a better mood," I cajoled.

I could tell she wanted to argue the point, but I slid my hand over her bottom. She was wearing a loose pair of sweatpants, and I promptly discovered she was also wearing no panties when my hand met the silky, soft skin of her bottom.

"Wyatt," she said weakly when I teased my fingers between her thighs from behind.

I slid one finger across her opening, which was slippery wet. "I'll let you do all the work, sweetheart."

"Wyatt..." she moaned when I sank two fingers inside her. She pushed back into my touch.

"Just ride me," I murmured as I dusted kisses on the back of her neck and pumped my fingers in and out of her tight little pussy.

A moment later, she sat astride me. I was so desperate for her that precum was already rolling out and down along my shaft.

"We're gonna have to make it quick, sweetheart. It's been too long," I rasped when she rose, and I positioned myself at her entrance.

She let out a satisfied little hum as she sank down over me. She gave me exactly what I wanted until she was crying out, and her pussy clenched around my cock. My release rushed through me like a fast storm.

Rosie curled against me, soft and warm, a few minutes later. I took a deep breath, letting it out with a sigh as I whispered, "I love you, Rosie."

She lifted her eyes to meet mine. "It's a good thing we never got divorced."

Chapter Thirty-Three

ROSIE

One year later

I smoothed my hands over my dress, nervous energy coursing through me. I reached up to adjust my hair. Fiona stopped behind me, resting her hands on my shoulders.

"You're already married. Just thought I might point that out," she said gently. When I met her gaze in the mirror, her lips curled in a small smile.

"You know what's crazy?" I asked.

"Uh, no," she said slowly.

"Wyatt and I got our marriage license in Vegas before we got drunk. You can't be obviously intoxicated, or they won't give you a license."

Her brows arched up. "Really?"

"It was a dare. I honestly didn't think we'd go through with it."

"Aren't you glad you went through with it?" Fiona asked as I turned away from the mirror.

"Absolutely."

"I have to say, you two are pretty good at keeping a secret."

I snorted a laugh. "No, we're not. Rhys knew the whole time."

Fiona rolled her eyes. "Rhys knows many things, I suspect." She studied me, her gaze sobering. "You look beautiful."

I smoothed my hands over my dress again. Wyatt and I were having an actual recommitment ceremony. We'd been married for a whole year now. Some days, I wondered why I hadn't grabbed that chance after our week together. I didn't recognize what we had then.

I took a shaky breath. McKenna came striding into the dressing room. She rested her hands on her hips. "You look amazing but nervous. You're already married. That might help with the nerves," she pointed out.

Fiona grinned over at her. "I just reminded her of the same thing."

"Is everything okay?" McKenna asked. "Are you and Wyatt falling apart, and you're just hiding it really well like you hid your wedding in Vegas?"

Her sarcastic question knocked me out of my anxiety, and I burst out laughing. "No! Everything is good. Really good. I just don't like being the center of attention. In fact, I hate it."

McKenna studied me for a beat. "You deserve to be celebrated." She swept into motion, herding me out of the dressing room and into the hallway. "Wyatt is already up front."

This whole thing had been Wyatt's idea. He'd told me that, even though we had a party to celebrate, he wanted to make sure I knew how important I was to him, so he wanted to do it all over.

Fiona's calming presence helped me as I waited.

We were having the ceremony outside at the harbor. As Wyatt had declared, "Church, or whatever. All that matters is you and me."

Moments later, I walked through the aisle between groups of chairs to where McKenna had created a beautiful arch of fireweed flowers twined together. A breeze gusted off the harbor. Wyatt was waiting, and when he turned to face me, my heart cracked wide open. Even now, a full year into this, I still got butterflies when I saw him. I was a little breathless as I met his eyes. His smile unfurled slowly, and my belly flipped. Tingles radiated through me, and I had to blink back tears when I stopped in front of him.

Thank God for friends. McKenna whisked the bouquet out of my hands. Wyatt's hands closed around mine, his grip warm and steadying. He didn't even wait to kiss me. He dipped and brushed his lips over mine, lingering for a moment before he lifted his head.

"I couldn't wait," he whispered.

Griffin chuckled from where he stood behind him.

Wyatt's eyes crinkled at the corners as he smiled. I told myself I would remember our vows this time because all I remembered from our first wedding were bits and pieces. Wyatt's eyes held mine throughout the ceremony, his gaze never wavering. When he said, "I do," my heart pounded with resounding beats, a sensation of openness and joy rushing through me.

He squeezed my hands when I made my promises to love him always, in all ways. Our second kiss was lingering. By the time he lifted his head, I was hot all over and completely breathless. I surprised myself when I felt tears hot on my cheeks, but he stepped close and pulled me into his arms.

"I love you, sweetheart," he murmured in my ear.

Yet again, he grounded me, reminding me of every-thing we had together.

When I leaned back, I heard McKenna's voice from behind me. "Jesus, you two will have to get a room. Oh, wait a minute, you already have a house together. Well, clearly, marriage agrees with you."

Wyatt smiled over at her. "It does."

EPILOGUE

Griffin Cannon

A few minutes earlier

My brother Wyatt held his wife's hands and looked deep into her eyes. "I do. I do," he repeated for good measure.

My throat was tight. I was happy, in a bone-deep way, for my twin brother. He'd crushed on Rosie for years before he'd been crazy enough to dare her to get a marriage license when they were in Las Vegas.

Roughly a year later, they were still happily married, but they were doing a recommitment ceremony. I glanced around the room to see plenty of teary eyes and lots of smiles. My mother had her palm pressed to her chest.

Rosie said her vows before Wyatt laid a deep kiss on her. The assembled group let up a small cheer. I clapped him on the shoulder a few moments later as he turned to hand me his jacket. He'd worn a suit and everything. He'd said he wanted to get this seriously right. Wyatt could be a tad superstitious.

"I'm happy for you," I said, leaning close to his ear.

He glanced over. "Yeah?"

"Well, I was already happy for you because you're already married," I teased. "But this is good. You wanted it, and Rosie wanted it, and Mom is beside herself. Now, make sure you keep treating Rosie right."

He flashed a quick grin before he turned his focus back to his beaming wife. The party swung into full gear. The ceremony was at the park down by the harbor. With it being summer, the weather was gorgeous. Of course, that wasn't always the case, but today, the weather obliged the ceremony with a bright blue sky, sun glittering on the water, and a soft, salty breeze coming off the harbor. The winery restaurant catered for the reception. Once the ceremony was over, food and drinks flowed.

Tourists milled about nearby as well. Fireweed Harbor was one of Southeast Alaska's popular travel spots. Boats rolled in and out of the harbor, both fishing and recreational. A raft of otters frolicked near the shoreline and a pair of curious seals watched us as they swam nearby.

"You're the only one left," my sister commented from my shoulder.

I glanced over at McKenna. "What do you mean?"

"You have to get married next."

I stared at her. "I'm in no hurry," I finally said.

McKenna took a bite of a crab puff. While she was chewing, I stole two of them and popped them in my mouth. "Wow, these are so good."

"Can't go wrong with Alaskan king crab and cream cheese," she said dryly. After finishing another crab puff, she added, "You should be."

"I should be what?" I countered.

"In more of a hurry to find someone. You're getting old, Griffin."

I eyed her. "I'm not old."

My sister rolled her eyes, just as our oldest brother Rhys stopped beside me.

"McKenna thinks I'm getting old," I said.

Rhys chuckled. "You're not."

Someone from the catering crew stopped by with a question for McKenna, and the party rolled along.

My eyes caught on a bright blue dress. When I turned, I realized the woman wearing it was a woman I'd encountered on the side of the highway once before. *Tish*. I hadn't forgotten her name. Awareness sizzled down my spine.

Her hair was pulled up in a tight bun. It was as if she was striving to give off an uptight librarian vibe. Her looks were understated. I couldn't forget her wide hazel eyes and full sensual mouth, though. My curiosity grew when I saw her say something to one of my brothers. When I headed in her direction, I was caught up in another conversation on the way over. By the time I looked up, she was out of sight.

The party rolled along, and I was just about to depart when there was a surprised scream. My reflexes kicked in, and I quickly followed the sound to realize it was coming from the dock at the harbor. There was a small commotion as I ran in the direction. I got to the edge of the dock and looked down to see Tish in the water, her blue dress billowing up on one side. Her head bobbed at the surface. I kicked off my shoes and stripped down to my briefs in a hot minute.

"My dress is caught on something," she called up. There was a thread of panic in her voice.

I was about to dive in when Wyatt reached my side. "You wait here. There must be a life buoy nearby if we need it. Find it," I barked in the general direction of my brother and the assembled group.

Alaskan waters were cold, even at the hottest time of year. We needed to get her out as fast as we could. You didn't swim or surf here without a wetsuit. Hypothermia could set in quickly based on the water temperature.

I braced myself for the jolt of cold as I broke through the surface. My system was electrified, instantly alive. I was close to Tish when I surfaced. "I'm stuck," she said, her teeth chattering.

"Kick off your shoes. I'll tear your dress," I ordered.

I dove under the surface quickly. The water blurred my vision, but I saw where her dress was hooked on one of the large bolts in the pilings. I didn't even know how she'd ended up in the water, but pondering that was for another time.

Her dress tore quickly with a good yank. Seconds later, I surfaced beside her and curled an arm around her waist. Her teeth were chattering harder.

"I know where the ladder is. Stay with me."

It was clear she could swim. Now that her dress was free, she kicked easily. I still kept my arm loosely gripped around her waist. I'd been a trained lifeguard back in high school.

Seconds later, we were at the ladder. She shook so hard from the cold, I was worried she might not be able to hold the ladder. I braced my arms around her. "Put your hands on the rungs."

While I was definitely cold, I hadn't been in the water as long as she had. I curled each of her hands around the ladder rungs. It was slow going, but she made it up even though she was shaking all over.

When we got to the top, Wyatt and Kenan were there on the docks and helped both of us up.

"We need blankets now," I barked out.

I lifted her in my arms and began striding down the dock. Someone from a nearby boat came clambering off with some towels and blankets. As I looked down into Tish's wide, frightened eyes, my heart gave a startling kick.

Thank you for reading Rosie & Wyatt's story! Want a glimpse of the future for them? Join my newsletter to receive an exclusive scene.

Sign up here: https://BookHip.com/LWBCKWJ

p.s. If you are already subscribed, you'll still be able to access the scene.

Up next is All The Afters, which kicks off my brand new firefighter series - Wild Fire Series!

I'm falling in love with a firefighter, and I'm pregnant.
Big problem: It's not his baby.

Griffin Cannon meets the woman of his dreams on the side of a deserted highway in Alaska. He figures he'll never see her again.

Until she ends up working for his brother. Things get complicated as fast as you can blink.

Don't miss Griffin & Tish's emotional, protective and swoony romance!

One-click: All The Afterss- available October 2024!!

For more swoony romance...

This Crazy Love kicks off the Swoon Series - small town southern romance with enough heat to melt you! Jackson & Shay's story is epic - swoon-worthy & intensely emotional. Jackson just happens to be Shay's brother's best friend. He's also *seriously* easy on the eyes. Shay has a past, the kind of past she would most definitely like to forget. Past or not, Jackson is about to rock her world. Don't miss their story!

Burn For Me is a second chance romance for the ages. Sexy firefighters? Check. Rugged men? Check. Wrapped up together? Check. Brave the fire in this hot, small-town romance. Amelia & Cade were high school sweethearts & then it all fell apart. When they cross paths again, it's epic - don't miss Cade's story!

For more small town romance, take a visit to Last Frontier Lodge in Diamond Creek. A sexy, alpha SEAL meets his match with a brainy heroine in Take Me Home. Marley is all brains & Gage is all brawn. Sparks fly when their worlds collide. Don't miss Gage & Marley's story!

If sports romance lights your spark, check out The Play. Liam is a British footballer who falls for Olivia, his doctor. A twist of forbidden heats up this swoon-worthy & laugh-out-loud romance. Don't miss Liam & Olivia's story.

ACKNOWLEDGMENTS

My gratitude for my readers is too big for words. Simply put, thank you from the bottom of my heart for giving me a reason to keep writing stories.

Much gratitude to my editor who patiently helps me with my stories and make sure I give my characters the best chance. My proofreader is ever-patient. Even I have given up on getting the days of the week straight in my stories, but she keeps me in line. Many thanks to my early readers who find any stubborn errors and cheer me on.

Najla Qamber keeps creating beautiful covers, each new one my latest favorite. So much gratitude to my assistant who helps me in more ways than I can count.

All my love to my family and my dogs.

xoxo

J.H. Croix

Fireweed Harbor Series

Make You Mine
Dare To Fall
Be The One
One More Time
Wait For You
Ever After All

Wild Fire Series

All The Afters - due out October 2024
When We Dare - due out January 2025

Light My Fire Series

Wild With You
Hold Me Now
Only Ever Us
Fall For Me
Keep Me Close
With Every Breath
All It Takes
Take Me Now
Meant To Be

Dare With Me Series

Crash Into You
Evers & Afters
Come To Me
Back To Us
Take Me There
After We Fall

Swoon Series

This Crazy Love
Wait For Me
Break My Fall
Truly Madly Mine
Still Go Crazy
If We Dare
Steal My Heart

Into The Fire Series
Burn For Me
Slow Burn
Burn So Bad
Hot Mess
Burn So Good
Sweet Fire
Play With Fire
Melt With You
Burn For You
Crash & Burn
That Snowy Night
Brit Boys Sports Romance
The Play
Big Win
Out Of Bounds
Play Me
Naughty Wish
Diamond Creek Alaska Novels
When Love Comes
Follow Love
Love Unbroken
Love Untamed
Tumble Into Love
Christmas Nights
Lodge Series
Take Me Home
Love at Last
Just This Once
Falling Fast
Stay With Me
When We Fall
Hold Me Close
Crazy For You
Just Us

9 781954 034976